Hans Andersen's Fairy Tales

Publisher's Note

Michael Foreman first composed his illustrations to these stories in 1976
when his publisher chose to align them with a translation by Erik Haugaard.
For the present edition a translation by Brian Alderson has been used with a
re-arranged sequencing of the stories. Earlier appearances of some of
his versions, together with his comments on sources, are
detailed in his Afterword on page 185.

A TEMPLAR BOOK

First published in the UK in 2013 by Templar Publishing,
an imprint of The Templar Company Limited,
Deepdene Lodge, Deepdene Avenue, Dorking, Surrey, RH5 4AT, UK
www.templarco.co.uk

'The Dung Beetle', 'The Little Mermaid', 'The Little Match-Girl', 'The Old House', 'The Red Shoes',
'The Ugly Duckling', 'The Wild Swans' and 'Thumbelina' translations copyright © 2013 by Brian Alderson
'The Snowman' and 'The Snow Queen: An Adventure in Seven Stories'
translations copyright © 1982 by Brian Alderson
'Big Claus and Little Claus', 'The Darning Needle', 'The Emperor's New Clothes', 'The Nightingale',
'The Princess and the Pea,' 'The Swineherd', 'The Steadfast Tin Soldier' and
'The Tinderbox' translations copyright © 1980 by Brian Alderson
Illustration copyright © 1976 by Michael Foreman

1 3 5 7 9 10 8 6 4 2

ISBN 978-1-84877-298-4

Printed and bound by Printing Express, Hong Kong

Hans Andersen's
Fairy Tales

templar publishing

CONTENTS

These translations are for
MARILYN
aller-kjærste Ven
B. A.

To my boys:
Mark, Ben and Jack
M. F.

LIST OF COLOUR PLATES

THE TINDERBOX

A soldier came marching along the road: one, two! one, two! He had his knapsack on his back and his sword by his side — for he'd been at the war and now he was off home. But then he met an old witch on the road — she was so ugly her lower lip hung right down to her chest.

She said, "Good evening, soldier! That's a fine sword and a big knapsack you've got there — you're a proper soldier, you are. Now you're going to get as much money as you want."

"Well I'll thank you for that, you old witch," said the soldier.

"D'you see that big tree?" said the witch, and pointed to a tree that stood near them. "That's all hollow inside. You must climb to the top where you'll see a hole that you can slide into and let yourself right down inside the tree. I'll tie a rope round your middle so that I can pull you out again when you call."

"So what'll I do down in the tree?" asked the soldier.

"Get money!" said the witch. "For you should know that when you get down to the bottom of the tree you'll be in a big passageway — all light, because there's more than a hundred lamps burning down there. Then you'll see three doors — you can open them because they've got keys in. If you go into the first room you'll see a big chest in the middle of the floor with a dog sitting on it. He's got eyes as big as a couple of teacups, but don't worry about that! I'll give you my blue-check apron and you can spread that out on the floor. Go up to the dog as quick as you like, put him on the apron, open the chest and take as many coins as you want. They're all copper; so if you'd rather have silver go into the next chamber – and there's a dog sitting there with eyes as big as a couple of mill-wheels. But don't you worry about that! Sit him on the apron and take the money. On the other hand, if you'd sooner have gold, you can do that too if you go into the third room. But the dog there, sitting on the money-chest, he's got eyes as big as round towers – he's a proper dog, for sure! But don't you worry about anything – just you sit him down on the apron and he won't do anything to you and you can take as much gold out of the chest as you want."

"That's not so bad," said the soldier. "But what am I going to give you, you old witch? You're not letting me have all this for nothing I'll be bound."

"No," said the witch. "I'll not take a single penny; just you bring me an old tinderbox that my grandmother forgot last time she was down there."

"Right-o, then! Tie the rope round my middle," said the soldier.

"Here it is," said the witch, "and here's my blue-check apron."

So the soldier climbed up into the tree, let himself down through the hole and found himself, just as the witch had said, in a big passageway where there were hundreds of lamps burning. He opened the first door. Ooh! There was the dog with eyes as big as teacups, and it stared at him.

"You're a nice fellow!" said the soldier and sat him down on the witch's apron and took just as many copper coins as he could get in his pockets. Then he closed the chest, put the dog back on it and went into the next chamber. Ay-a! There was the dog with the eyes as big as mill-wheels.

"Don't you stare so hard at me," said the soldier, "you'll strain your eyes!", and he sat the dog on the witch's apron, but when he saw so much silver in the chest, he threw away the copper money and filled his pockets and his knapsack just with silver. Then he went into the third room. Oh, that was horrible! The dog in there really did have eyes as big as round towers – and they went round in his head like wheels!

"Good evening," said the soldier and touched his cap, for he'd never seen a dog like this before. But after he'd looked at him for a bit he thought, "That'll do", and he lifted him on to the floor and opened up the chest. Now God preserve us! What

There was the dog with the eyes as big as mill-wheels

a lot of gold! He could have bought the whole of Copenhagen, the cake-woman's sugar pigs, and all the tin soldiers, whips and rocking-horses in the whole world! Yes – that was money all right! – and the soldier threw out all the silver shillings that he'd put in his pockets and his knapsack and took the gold instead – yes, indeed, pockets, knapsack, cap, boots, they were all so full that he could hardly walk. Now he'd really got some money! He sat the dog back on the chest, closed the door and called up through the tree, "Pull me up, you old witch!"

"Have you got the tinderbox?" she asked.

"That's a point," said the soldier, "I clean forgot it," and he went back and found it. Then the witch pulled him up and he was back on the road again with his pockets and his boots and his knapsack and his cap all full of money.

"Now, what do you want with this tinderbox?" asked the soldier.

"That's nothing to do with you," said the witch, "you've got all your money. Just give me the tinderbox."

"Snick, snack!" said the soldier. "If you don't tell me straight away what you want with it I'll draw my sword and chop your head off!"

"No!" said the witch.

So the soldier chopped her head off! There she lay. But he just tied up all the money in her apron, took it on his back like a bundle, put the tinderbox in his pocket and went off to the town.

That was a fine town, and he put up at the finest inn and called for the very best room and food that they had, for now, with all that money, he was a rich man.

To the servant who had to clean his boots it seemed that these were remarkably old boots for such a rich gentleman – but then he hadn't bought any new ones yet. The next day he got proper boots and clothes to match! So now the soldier had become a respectable gentleman and they told him all about the sights of the town and about the king and about what a pretty princess he had for a daughter.

"How do you get to see her?" asked the soldier.

"She's not to be seen at all," said everyone. "She lives in a big copper castle with lots of walls and towers round it. Nobody but the king is allowed to go in or out because it's been foretold that she'll be married to a common soldier and the king can't bear the thought of it."

"Well I'd certainly like to see her," thought the soldier, "but they just wouldn't allow it."

From now on he began to live a merry life. He went to the theatre, drove in the royal park and gave away lots of money to the poor. And that was very kind of him – because he knew from the old days what a nasty thing it was to be without even a penny. He was so rich – had such fine clothes, and so many friends that they all said, 'Here was a rare 'un, a real gentleman' – and that was something the soldier liked to hear. But since he spent out his money every day and never got any back again, the time eventually arrived when he only had tuppence left and he had to move from the smart room where he lived to a tiny little garret under the roof. And he had to clean his boots himself, and mend them with a darning-needle, and none of his friends came to see him because there were too many stairs.

One evening when it was getting dark and he hadn't the money to buy himself a light, he remembered that there was a little stump of candle in the tinderbox that he'd taken from the hollow tree where the witch had helped him down. He fetched out the tinderbox and the candle-end, but just as he struck a light, with sparks flying from the flint, the door sprang open and the dog with eyes as big as teacups – that he'd seen below the tree – stood there in front of him and said, "What does my lord command?"

"What's all this?" said the soldier. "That's a very fancy tinderbox if I can get whatever I like with it. Bring me some money!" he said to the dog, and *whizz!* he was gone, and *whizz!* he was back again, with a huge bagful of pennies in his mouth.

Now the soldier realised what a beautiful tinderbox that was! If he struck it once along came the dog that sat on the chest of copper coins; if he struck it twice, along came the one with the silver coins and if he struck it three times, it was the one with gold. So the soldier moved back to the smart room again, went about in fine clothes, and straight away all his friends recognised him again and said what a fine fellow he was.

Once again he started thinking, that's a remarkable thing that no one can get to see the princess. Everyone says she must be very beautiful, but what's the good of that if she has to spend all her time in a big copper castle with all those towers! Couldn't I get to see her? What about my tinderbox? And so he struck a light and – *whizz!* – there was the dog with eyes as big as teacups.

"Well it may be the middle of the night," said the soldier, "but I'd very much like to see the princess. Just for a moment."

So the dog ran straight out the door, and before the soldier could think about it he was back again with the princess. She sat on the dog's back, asleep, and she was so beautiful that anyone could see that she was a real princess; the soldier couldn't help it: he had to kiss her, for he was a proper soldier.

Then the dog ran back again with the princess, but when the morning came and the king and queen were pouring out their tea the princess said that she'd dreamed such a strange dream during the night about a dog and a soldier. She'd ridden on the dog and the soldier had kissed her.

"Oh, that's a fine story!" said the queen.

Now, next night, one of the old ladies-in-waiting was told to stay by the princess's bed to see if it really was a dream or if it could be something else.

As for the soldier, he was longing dreadfully to see the beautiful princess again, and so the dog came in the night, took her up and ran off as fast as he could. But the old lady-in-waiting put on her wellingtons and ran after him just as quickly. When she saw the two of them go into a big house she thought: now I know where it is, and she made a big cross on the door with a piece of chalk. Then she went home to bed and the dog brought the princess back again. But when he saw that a cross had been chalked on the door where the soldier lived, he took another bit of chalk and put crosses on every door in the town. That was a clever piece of work, since it meant that the lady-in-waiting couldn't find the right door because there was a cross on all of them.

Early in the morning the king, the queen, the old lady-in-waiting and all the household cavalry came to see where the princess had been. "Here it is!" said the king, for he saw the first door with a cross on it. "No, my dear, here it is!" said the queen, who saw the next door with a cross on it. "But here's one, and here's one!" said everybody, for wherever they looked they saw crosses on the doors. So now they could see that it wasn't going to be much help going on searching.

But the queen was a very clever lady who could do more than just ride in a carriage. She took her big gold scissors and cut up a large bit of silk into pieces and sewed a neat little bag. Then she filled it with small, fine grains of buckwheat, tied it on to the princess's back and, when that was done, she cut a little hole in the bag so that the grains would drop out wherever the princess went.

That night the dog came again, took the princess on his back and ran to the soldier with her, for he loved her very much and wished for all the world that he was a prince so that he could marry her.

The dog never noticed how the grains of wheat dropped out, leading from the castle to the soldier's window, just where he ran up the wall with the princess. In the morning the king and the queen could see where their daughter had been, so they took the soldier and put him in prison.

There he sat. Ooh, how dark and uncomfortable it was! And they said to him, "You'll hang in the morning." That wasn't very funny, and, what's more, he'd left his tinderbox back home at the inn.

Next morning he could see through the iron bars of his little window all the people hurrying through the town to see him hang. He heard the trumpets and saw the soldiers marching. Everyone was running out, and among them there was a shoemaker's boy with his apron and slippers on. He went charging by so quickly that one of his slippers flew off and came to land by the wall where the soldier sat peering through his iron bars.

"Hi! You cobbler-boy — you needn't be in such a hurry!" said the soldier. "They can't do anything till I get there! But would you like to run back to where I used to live and fetch me my tinderbox? If you do, I'll give you fourpence — but you'll have to pick your feet up!" Well the cobbler's boy was all for having fourpence and he tore back for the tinderbox, gave it to the soldier and — now we'll hear what happened!

Outside the town they'd put up a tall gallows, with soldiers standing round and hundreds and thousands of people. The king and the queen sat on a beautiful throne across from the judges and all the council.

The soldier was already standing on the ladder, but when they came to put the rope round his neck, he said that surely a condemned man was always granted one last innocent wish before he met his punishment. For his part he'd really like to smoke a pipe of tobacco, since it was the last pipe he'd have in the world.

Well, the king wouldn't say no to that, so the soldier took out his tinderbox and struck a light: one, two, three! And there stood all the dogs — the one with eyes as big as teacups, the one with eyes as big as mill-wheels and the one with eyes as big as round towers.

"Help me now so that I don't get hanged!" said the soldier, so the dogs fell on the judges and all the council, and took one by the leg and one by the nose and threw them all miles up in the air so that they fell down and broke in pieces.

"I won't be thrown!" said the king, but the biggest dog took him, and the queen and threw them after the others. Then the king's soldiers were afraid and all the people shouted out, "Little soldier, you must be king and have the beautiful princess!"

So the soldier sat in the king's carriage and all the dogs pranced around in front shouting, "Hurrah!" and the boys whistled through their fingers and the soldiers presented arms. The princess came out of the copper castle and became queen, which she liked very much. The wedding lasted a week and the dogs sat up at the table and made big eyes!

LITTLE CLAUS AND BIG CLAUS

There were two men living in one village and they both had the same name; both of them were called Claus. But one had four horses and the other had only one horse — and so that you could tell each from the other, the man with four horses was called Big Claus and the man with only one horse was called Little Claus.

Now we're going to hear what happened to the two of them, for this is a true story!

The whole week through Little Claus had to do the ploughing for Big Claus and lend him his one horse; then Big Claus would help him with his four, but that was only once a week — on Sunday. *Huzza!* How Little Claus cracked his whip over all those five horses, for on that one day they were as good as his. The sun shone so kindly and all the bells in the church-steeples were ringing; people were all dressed up and went along with their hymn books under their arms to hear the parson preaching; and they'd see Little Claus ploughing with his five horses, and he'd be so merry that he'd crack his whip over and over again and call out, "Heigh-up all my horses!"

"You mustn't say that," said Big Claus, "only one of the horses is yours!"

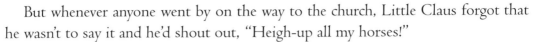

But whenever anyone went by on the way to the church, Little Claus forgot that he wasn't to say it and he'd shout out, "Heigh-up all my horses!"

"Well now, I must ask you to stop that," said Big Claus, "for if you say it just once more I'll give your horse such a crack on the head that he'll fall down dead on the spot and that'll be the end of him!"

"Well I certainly won't say it any more," said Little Claus — but as people went by, nodding 'good day' to him, he felt so happy and he thought it looked so good, him with the five horses ploughing his field, that he cracked his whip and shouted, "Heigh-up all my horses!"

"I'll give your horse 'heigh-up'!" said Big Claus, and he picked up a mallet and hit Little Claus's one and only horse on the forehead so that he fell down stone dead.

"Aaah! Now I haven't got any horse at all!" said Little Claus, and he started to cry. Then he flayed the horse, took the hide and let it dry in the wind, and then put it in a bag, slung it over his shoulder and went into the town to sell it for leather.

He had a long way to go, needing to pass through a huge, dark wood, and the weather turned frightful. He went altogether astray and before he could get right again it was evening, and he was too far off either to get to the town or to get back home before nightfall.

Hard by the wayside there lay a big farmhouse, with shutters closed over the windows, but you could still see some light shining out through the top. "I may well be allowed to spend the night there," thought Little Claus, and he went and knocked.

The farmer's wife opened the door, but when she heard what he wanted she told him to be off; her man wasn't at home and she wasn't inclined to take in strangers.

"Well then, I shall have to lie down outside," said Little Claus, and the farmer's wife shut the door in his face.

Nearby there stood a large haystack and between this and the house there was a little shed with a flat roof thatched with straw.

"I can lie down up there," said Little Claus when he saw the roof, "that's a nice bed — only I hope the stork won't come and bite my legs off" (for a real live stork was standing up there on the roof where he had his nest).

So Little Claus climbed up onto the shed where he lay down and wriggled himself about to get comfortable. The wooden shutters over the windows weren't closed at the top and so he could see right into the room. There was a huge table laid in there, with wine and roast beef and really beautiful fish. The farmer's wife and the parish

"I'll give your horse 'heigh up'!" said Big Claus

clerk sat at the table by themselves and she kept filling his glass and he carved into the fish, for that was what he liked best of all.

"Oh! If only I could get some too!" said Little Claus and he stretched out his head to peer through the window. Good heavens! What a gorgeous cake he could see in there. My word, that was a feast! Then he heard someone riding down the road towards the house. It was the woman's husband coming home.

This husband was a good enough fellow but he had one odd peculiarity: he couldn't stand the sight of parish clerks — whenever he laid eyes on parish clerks he went wild. This was the reason why the parish clerk had called in to say good day to the woman just then, for he'd seen that her man wasn't at home, and the good woman, for her part, had put out the best of everything for him. Now though, when they heard the husband coming back, they were frightened out of their wits and the woman told the clerk to climb into a huge chest that stood in the corner — which he did, for he knew well enough that the man couldn't stand the sight of parish clerks. The woman quickly stowed all the fancy meat and wine away in her oven, for if her husband had seen all that he'd have been certain to ask what it was all about.

"Ah, dearie me!" sighed Little Claus up on his shed when he saw all the food put away.

"Is there somebody up there?" asked the farmer, looking up at Little Claus. "What do you think you're doing lying up there? Better come indoors with me!" So Little Claus told him how he'd lost his way and asked him if he could stay the night there.

"Certainly, certainly," said the farmer, "but first of all we must have something to eat."

The woman greeted them both in the friendliest fashion, set out a long table and served them up a great bowl of porridge. The farmer was famished and tucked in with a great appetite, but Little Claus couldn't help thinking about the delicious roast and fish and cake that he knew were inside the oven.

Under the table, by his feet, he'd laid his bag with the horse-hide in it (for we know — don't we? — that he'd left home to sell this in the town). Well he didn't care at all for the porridge, so he trod, up and down, on the bag and the dry hide there creaked pretty loud. "Shush!" said Little Claus to his bag, but at the same time he trod on it again so that it creaked even louder.

"Hey there! What have you got in that bag?" asked the farmer.

"Oh — that's a wizard!" said Little Claus. "He says that we're not to eat porridge

for he's conjured up a whole oven full of roast beef and fish and cake."

"What on earth's that?!" said the farmer and opened the oven quick and saw all the good food that his wife had hidden there, but which he thought had been conjured up by the wizard in the bag. The woman didn't dare say anything, but straight away put the food on the table and the two of them ate up the fish, the meat and the cake. Then Little Claus trod on his bag so that the hide creaked.

"What does he say now?" asked the farmer.

"He says," said Little Claus, "that he's also conjured up three bottles of wine for us, and they're in the oven too." So the woman had to bring out the wine that she'd hidden and the farmer drank it and grew very merry; it seemed to him that it would be very nice to own a wizard like the one Little Claus had in his bag.

"Can he conjure up the Devil too?" asked the farmer. "I'd like to see something like that now that I'm feeling so cheerful."

"Yes indeed," said Little Claus, "my wizard can do whatever I want him to – can't you?" he asked, and trod on the hide so that it creaked. "Can you hear? He said, 'Yes.' But he says the Devil looks so ugly that we'd better not look at him."

"Oh, I'm not scared! What does he look like anyway?"

"Well – he's the spitting image of the parish clerk."

"Ho!" said the farmer. "That is ugly! You ought to know that I can't stand the sight of parish clerks; but it doesn't matter now – since I know he's the Devil, I'll be able to bear it. I'm ready for him, but he'd better not come too near me!"

"Well I'll ask my wizard," said Little Claus, treading on the bag and listening.

"What's he saying?"

"He says you can go over there and open the chest in the corner and you'll see the Devil crouching down inside, but you'd better hold on to the lid so that he doesn't slip out."

"Will you help me hold on to it then?" asked the farmer and went over to the chest where his wife had hidden the real parish clerk, who was sitting inside trembling with fear.

The farmer lifted the lid a little and peeped inside: "Hoo!" he shrieked and jumped backwards. "Yes! Now I've seen him and he looks just like our clerk! Oh! It's terrible!"

So that meant they had to have a drink, and they went on drinking far into the night.

"You'll have to sell me that wizard," said the farmer. "You can ask as much as you like for him. Go on — I'll give you a whole bushel of money straight away!"

"No, I can't do that," said Little Claus, "just you think what I can get with a wizard like that!"

"Aw, I want him real bad," said the farmer, and went on asking and pleading.

"Oh, very well," said Little Claus in the end, "since you've been so kind as to put me up for the night it makes no matter. You can have the wizard for a bushel of money — but it had better be full up to the top."

"It's all yours," said the farmer, "but you must take that chest over there with you; I'll not have it in the house a minute more — how do I know that he isn't still in there?"

Little Claus gave the farmer his bag with the flayed hide in and got a whole bushel of money for it — and that filled up to the top. The farmer gave him a big barrow too, to cart off the money and the chest.

"Goodbye," said Little Claus, and he went off with the money and the big chest — with the parish clerk still inside.

On the other side of the wood there was a great, deep river with the current running so strongly that you could scarcely make headway against it. They'd built a big new bridge over it, and Little Claus stopped in the middle of this and said out loud, so that the parish clerk could hear inside the chest, "Now — what on earth shall I do with this stupid chest? It's so heavy you'd think it was full of stones. I shall just wear myself out if I lug it any further — I'll throw it in the river and if it sails home to me, that's fine, and if it doesn't, well who cares!"

So he put one hand under the chest and lifted it up a little as if he was going to throw it in the water.

"No! Leave off!" shouted the parish clerk in the chest. "Let me get out first!"

"Hoo!" said Little Claus, pretending to be scared out of his wits. "He's still in there! I must throw him in the river quick and drown him."

"No! Oh, no!" shouted the parish clerk. "I'll give you a whole bushel of money if you'll leave off!"

"Well — that's another story," said Little Claus, and opened the chest. The parish clerk crawled out straight away, pushed the empty chest into the water and went off home where Little Claus got a whole bushel of money. So, what with the bushel he had from the farmer, his barrow was now full up with money!

"Look at that — I'm well enough paid for my horse!" he said to himself when he got home to his room and emptied all the money out into a great heap in the middle of the floor. "That'll make Big Claus cross when he gets to hear how rich I've got through my one horse — but I'll not tell him just now." And he sent a boy to Big Claus to ask the loan of a bushel measure.

"What does he want with that?" thought Big Claus, and he smeared some tar on the bottom so that a bit of whatever was measured would stick to it — and so it came about, for when he got the measure back, there on the bottom were three new silver shillings.

"What's all this?" said Big Claus and ran straight off to the Little one. "Where did you get all that money from?"

"Oh, that was for my horse's hide that I sold yesterday evening."

"Well that's good money and no mistake," said Big Claus and he ran straight home, took an axe and hit all his four horses on the head, flayed them and carted off their skins to the town.

"Hides! Hides! Who'll buy my hides?" he shouted up and down the streets.

All the shoemakers and tanners came running out and asked what he wanted for them.

"A bushel of money for each," said Big Claus.

"Are you daft?" they all said. "Do you think we've got money by the bushel?"

"Hides! Hides! Who'll buy my hides?" he shouted again, but when they asked him how much his hides cost he always answered, "A bushel of money."

"He's trying to make fools of us," they all said, and the shoemakers took their straps and the tanners their leather aprons and they began to beat Big Claus. "Hides! Hides!" they jeered at him. "Oh, yes! We'll give you a hide that'll spit red pigs! Out of the town with him!" they shouted, and Big Claus had to skip off as quick as he could — he'd never had a thrashing like that!

"Now," he said when he got home, "Little Claus'll pay for this; I'll kill him for it!"

But back at Little Claus's place his old grandmother had died. In her time she'd been harsh and cruel to him right enough, but he was still very sorry and he took the dead old lady and laid her in his warm bed to see if she'd come to life again. That's where she was to lie all night long, and as for him, he'd sit in the corner and sleep on

a stool, which he'd done often enough before.

Well – while he was sitting there in the night, the door opened and in came Big Claus with his axe. He already knew where Little Claus's bed was and he went straight up to it and hit the dead grandmother on the head, for he thought she was Little Claus.

"There you are," he said, "you'll not make a fool of me again," and he went back home.

"What a wicked, evil fellow that is!" said Little Claus. "He was out to kill me. It's a good thing the old lady was already dead or he'd have killed her!"

And he dressed his old grandmother in her Sunday best, borrowed a horse from his neighbour, harnessed it to a wagon and put his old grandmother in the back seat so that she shouldn't fall out when he drove along, and in this way they trundled through the wood. At sunrise they found themselves outside a big inn and here Little Claus pulled up and went inside for something to eat.

Now the innkeeper was a man with lots and lots of money, and he was a good fellow too, but he had a pretty hot temper, as though someone had filled him up with pepper and tobacco.

"Good morning," he said to Little Claus, "you've got your Sunday clothes on very early today."

"Yes," said Little Claus, "I'm off to town with my old grandmother – she's sitting in the wagon outside. I can't bring her in the room here. Would you like to take her a glass of mead – but you'll have to shout at her, she's rather hard of hearing."

"Certainly, I'll do that," said the innkeeper, and he poured out a great glass of mead and took it out to the dead grandmother who was propped up in the wagon.

"Here's a glass of mead from your grandson," said the innkeeper – but the dead woman didn't say a word, just sat there all quiet...

"Don't you hear?" shouted the innkeeper as loud as he could. "Here's a glass of mead from your grandson!"

Once again he shouted the same thing, and yet again, but since she never stirred from the spot he lost his temper and threw the glass in her face so that the mead ran down over her nose and she fell backwards into the wagon, for she was only propped up, not fastened.

"Hey, hey, hey!" shouted Little Claus, leaping out of the door and grabbing the innkeeper by the throat. "Now you've killed my grandmother! Just look – there's a great big hole in her forehead!"

"Oh, what a calamity!" cried the innkeeper, wringing his hands. "That's all because of my bad temper! Dear old Little Claus, I'll give you a whole bushel of money and have your grandmother buried just like my own – but don't say a word, or else they'll chop my head off and that's a very painful thing to happen."

So Little Claus got another bushel of money and the innkeeper buried the old grandmother as though she were his own.

Once Little Claus got home again with all this money, he sent his boy straight over to Big Claus to ask him for the loan of his bushel measure.

"What's all this?" said Big Claus. "Haven't I just killed him! I must go and see for myself!" So he went over himself with the measure to see Little Claus.

"Now where have you got all that money from?" he asked, opening his eyes wide at the sight of all that Little Claus had come by.

"That was my grandmother and not me that you just killed," said Little Claus, "so I've sold her and got a bushel of money for her."

"Well that's good money and no mistake," said Big Claus and hurried home, took an axe and straight away killed his old grandmother. He laid her in a wagon, drove into the town where the apothecary lived and asked him if he'd like to buy a dead person.

"Who is it, and where does it come from?" asked the apothecary.

"It's my grandmother," said Big Claus. "I've just killed her and she's yours for a bushel of money!"

"Lord save us!" said the apothecary. "You talk too much! Don't go around saying things like that – that's the way to lose your head!" And he told him straight out what a dreadful thing he'd done, and what a wicked man he was, and how he must be punished. Big Claus was so frightened that he leapt out of the apothecary's and into his wagon, whipped up his horses and drove home. But the apothecary and everyone else thought he was mad, and left him to drive where he would.

"You'll pay for this!" said Big Claus, out on the high-road. "Yes, you'll pay for this, Little Claus!" As soon as he got home he took the biggest sack he could find, went over to Little Claus and said, "Well – you've made a fool of me again. First I killed my horses, then my old grandmother. That's all your fault – but you'll not make a fool of me any more." And he seized Little Claus round his middle and put him in the sack. Then he took him up on his back and called out, "Now I'm going to drown you!"

He had a long way to go before he came to the river and Little Claus was not all that easy to carry. The road ran close by the church, with the organ playing and the people inside singing so beautifully that Big Claus put down his sack with Little Claus inside close by the church door and thought that it might do him a power of good if, first of all, he went in and listened to a psalm before he went any further. Little Claus couldn't get out and all the people were in church so Big Claus went in.

"Oh dear, oh dear," sighed Little Claus inside the sack. He twisted and he turned but it was impossible for him to loosen the fastening. At the same time, though, an old drover came along, a man with snow-white hair and a big stick in his hand. He was driving a whole herd of cows and bulls in front of him and they ran against the sack with Little Claus inside so that it overturned.

"Oh dear," sighed Little Claus, "I'm so young, but even so I'm bound for heaven!"

"And what about poor me?" said the drover. "So old and can't get there."

"Open up the sack," called Little Claus. "You creep inside instead of me. That way you'll get straight to heaven!"

"Yes – I'll be glad to do it," said the drover, and he unloosed the sack for Little Claus, who jumped out at once.

"Will you look after my cattle?" said the old man, and he crept into the sack which Little Claus tied up before making off down the road with all the cows and bulls.

Soon afterwards Big Claus came out of the church. He took the sack up on his back again and it seemed to him that it had got lighter, for the old drover was no more than half the weight of Little Claus. "How easy he is to carry now! That's what comes of listening to a psalm!" And he went on to the river, which was broad and deep, and he threw the sack with the old drover inside into the water, calling out after it (for he thought Little Claus was still in there), "Now then, you'll not make a fool of me any more!"

Then he set off for home, but when he got to a place where two roads crossed he met Little Claus and all his cattle.

"What's all this?" said Big Claus. "Haven't I just drowned you?"

"Why yes!" said Little Claus. "You threw me in the river about half an hour ago."

"Well where did you get all those fine beasts from then?" asked Big Claus.

"Oh, they're sea-cattle," said Little Claus. "I'll tell you the whole story – and, what's more, I'll thank you for drowning me. I fell on my feet, so to say. I'm really rich now! I was so terrified when I lay in that sack, and the wind whistled round my ears when you threw me off that bridge into the cold water. I sank straight to the bottom, but I didn't hurt myself because there's the most beautiful soft grass growing down there. I fell on that and straight away the bag was opened and a beautiful girl in a snow-white dress with a green garland in her wet hair took me by the hand and said, "Is that you, Little Claus? Here are some cattle to be going on with; a mile further down the road there's a whole herd more, and I'll give those to you too." And then I saw that the river was a great highway for the sea-folk. They walked around and drove their wagons on the bottom, from the sea right inland to where the river ends. It was so beautiful down there with the flowers and fresh grass and fishes swimming in the water and darting past your ears just like birds in the air. Oh there were fine folk down there and such cattle grazing along the hedges and ditches!"

"Well why ever did you come back to us again?" asked Big Claus. "I'd never have done that if it's so beautiful down there!"

"Ah yes," said Little Claus, "well that's just where I've been clever. You heard how I said that the sea-maiden told me 'a mile down the road' there was 'a whole herd of cattle' for me (and by 'road' she meant 'river', for you can't go anywhere else). Well — I know how the river bends — in here, and out there   it's a long way round. No — it's much shorter, if you can do it, to come up on land here and drive across to the river again. That way I save about half a mile and get to my sea-cattle that much quicker!"

"Oh, you're a lucky fellow!" said Big Claus. "Do you think I can get some sea-cattle too if I go to the bottom of the river?"

"Yes — I should think so!" said Little Claus. "But I can't carry you to the river in a sack, you're too heavy for me. But if you'll go over there yourself and squeeze into a bag, I'll throw you in with pleasure."

"Well, thanks very much," said Big Claus, "but if I don't get any sea-cattle when I'm down there then I'll beat you for it, you may be sure."

"Oh, come, come — don't be so nasty!" and so together they went across to the river. When the cattle, who were thirsty, saw the water, they ran as fast as they could to get themselves a drink.

"Just look how they're rushing," said Little Claus, "they want to get back to the bottom again."

"Well you help me first," said Big Claus, "otherwise I'll beat you," and he squeezed himself into the big sack which they'd laid across the back of one of the bullocks. "Put a stone in too, for fear that I don't sink," said Big Claus.

"That'll be all right," said Little Claus, but he put a large stone in the sack all the same. Then he tied it up tight with the rope and gave it a good push: *Plump!* There went Big Claus into the river and straight away sank to the bottom.

"I'm afraid he won't find the cattle," said Little Claus, and he drove the ones that he had back home.

THE PRINCESS ON THE PEA

There was once a prince who wanted a princess, but she had to be a *real* princess. So he travelled round the whole world to find just such a one — but everywhere there was something wrong. Certainly, there were plenty of princesses, but he could never quite make up his mind if they were real princesses, for there was always something that didn't seem quite right about them. So he came home again, all sad, because he wanted to have a true princess.

One evening a fearful storm blew up — thunder, lightning, rain streaming down — it was absolutely terrible! Then there came a knocking on the town gate and the old king went down himself to open it.

It was a princess, standing out there. But, goodness gracious, what a sight she was in the rain and the storm! The water ran down her hair and down her clothes, and it ran into the toes of her shoes and out at the heels, and yet she said she was a true princess.

"Huh, we'll soon see about that!" thought the old queen, but she didn't say it out loud. She just went into the bedchamber, took off all the bed-clothes and put a pea on the bottom of the bedstead. Then she took twenty mattresses and put them on

Only a true princess could have such delicate skin

top of the pea, and then she put twenty eiderdown quilts on top of the mattresses.

That's where the princess had to lie all that night.

Next morning they asked her how she'd slept.

"Oh, it was terrible," said the princess. "I hardly shut my eyes the whole night long! God knows what was in my bed. There was something so hard in there that I'm black and blue all over. It really was absolutely terrible!"

So they could see that she was a real princess, because she'd felt the pea through those twenty mattresses and twenty eiderdown quilts. Only a true princess could have such delicate skin.

The prince took her for his queen, for now he knew that she was a real princess, and the pea ended up in the art gallery where you can still see it, unless someone's taken it away.

There now — that was a real story.

THUMBELINA

Once upon a time there was a woman who wanted to have a child but she didn't know where to get one from. So she went to an old witch and said, "I so badly want to have a little child; can you tell me at all where I can get one from?"

"We should be able to manage that," said the witch. "Here's a barleycorn. It's not the sort that a farmer plants in his fields or that the chickens get to eat, but just you put it in a flower-pot and you'll see what you will see."

"Well, many thanks," said the woman and she gave the witch sixty pence, went home and planted the barleycorn. Pretty soon it sprouted into a large and handsome flower, a bit like a tulip, but with its leaves tightly closed as though it were in bud. "It's a beautiful flower," said the woman and she kissed its shapely red and yellow leaves. But just as she kissed them the flower gave a loud 'pop' and opened. Now you could see that it really was a tulip but there, sitting among the green stamens at its centre, was a little girl — a little girl, delicate and finely-proportioned, and hardly bigger than your thumb. So they called her Thumbelina.

A varnished walnut shell made a nice cradle for her with blue-violet leaves for a mattress and a rose leaf for a coverlet. That did for the nights, but during the day she was on the table where the woman had put a soup-plate with a garland of flowers round the edge, their stalks in the water, and here Thumbelina could sit and float on a large tulip leaf, rowing herself from one side of the soup-plate to the other with a pair of white horsehair oars. It really looked very pretty and she'd sing more sweetly and charmingly than you'd ever heard before.

One night, as she lay in her comfy bed, a hideous toad hopped in at the window through a broken pane. It was big, it was ugly, it was wet, and it hopped over to the table where Thumbelina was sleeping under her rose-leaf quilt.

"Now that would make a nice wife for my son," said the toad and it picked up the walnut shell where Thumbelina was sleeping and hopped back through the broken pane into the garden. Here a big, broad stream flowed by, but its bank was all swampy and muddy and it was there that the toad lived with her son. Oogh! He was just as nasty and horrible as his mother. *"Cloaca! Cloaca! Rek-kek-kek-kex!"* was all he had to say when he saw the pretty little girl in her walnut-shell bed.

"Don't make such a row, or you'll wake her," said the mother toad. "She might well get away from us for she's as light as swansdown. We'll stick her out in the stream on one of those big water-lily leaves and it'll be like a little island for her. She won't be able to get off it while we smarten up that little boudoir down in the mud where you can both live and look after yourselves."

Out in the stream there were dozens of water-lilies with broad green leaves that looked as though they were floating on the water. The one that was furthest out was also the biggest and that's where the old toad swam out to, with Thumbelina in her walnut-shell cradle. The poor little thing woke up early in the morning and when she saw where she was she began to cry bitterly, for there was water all round her big green leaf and no way for her to get back to land.

The mother toad was down in the mud, prettying up the boudoir with rushes and yellow lilies (it was going to be really smart for her new daughter-in-law) and then she swam out with her horrible son to the lily-leaf where Thumbelina lay. They wanted to take her nice little bed to set up in the bridal chamber before she went there herself. The old toad bowed down before her in the water and said, "This is my son who's to be your husband. I know you're both going to live so happily down there in the mud."

"Cloaca! Cloaca! Rek-kek-kek-kex!" was all that the son had to say.

Then they took her nice little bed and swam off with it; but Thumbelina sat alone on her green leaf, weeping, because she certainly didn't want to live down there with the ugly toad and have her hateful son for a husband.

Some little fish that were swimming in the water below her had seen the toad and heard what she said. So they stuck their heads up to take a look at the little girl and as soon as they'd done that they realised that she was so pretty that it would be shameful for her to be stuck with that horrible toad. No, no, no – quite unthinkable. So they got together round the green stalk of the lily where she was standing and gnawed away at it with their teeth until the leaf floated away into the stream, carrying Thumbelina where the toad would never catch her. Away she went, past many new places, with the birds in their bushes singing "Pretty, pretty, little 'Lina" and the leaf carrying her further and further into the countryside.

A pretty little white butterfly came flying round her and eventually settled on the leaf for he liked the look of Thumbelina, who was so pleased to be rid of the toad and floating along with the sun shining golden on the water. She took off the ribbon that was round her waist and tied one end to the butterfly and the other to the leaf so that they sailed much faster, with her balancing on it as it went along.

At that moment a big cockchafer came flying by. He spotted her and straight away clutched his claws round her slender waist and carried her up into a tree, leaving the lily-leaf to travel on up the stream with the butterfly unable to get loose. Thumbelina may have been terrified as the cockchafer carried her up to the tree-top, but she was also overcome with sorrow at tying the butterfly to the leaf – if he couldn't get loose, he'd surely starve to death.

But that meant nothing to the cockchafer. He sat down with her on the biggest green leaf of the tree, gave her a sweet part of the blossom to eat and remarked that although she wasn't a cockchafer, she was a very pretty creature. Then all the other cockchafers who lived in the tree came to pay a visit. They looked Thumbelina over and the lady cockchafers shook their feelers and said, "Why, she's only got two legs – how pitiful!" "She's not got any feelers!" they said. "Look at her waist," they said, "it's so titchy that she could even be a human. She's just ugly." That's what the lady cockchafers said – even though she was so pretty!

She'd certainly seemed so to the cockchafer who'd brought her along, but since all the others said she was ugly he thought so too and decided he'd have nothing more to do with her. She could go where she liked. He flew her down from the tree and

They sailed much faster, with her balancing on it as it went along

put her on a daisy and she cried that she was so ugly that the cockchafers didn't want her — and yet she was the most beautiful person you could think of — as fine and pure as the most beautiful rose.

All summer through, poor little Thumbelina lived all on her own in the great wood. She wove herself a bed out of sheaves of grass and hung it up under a big burdock leaf as a shelter from the rain. She drew nectar from the flowers for food and every morning drank the dew that had gathered in the leaves. And so the summer passed, and then the autumn, but then the winter came, the long, cold winter. All the birds that had sung so sweetly for her took flight; the trees and the flowers shed their leaves; the big burdock under which she had sheltered shrivelled up into a withered yellow stalk; and she got bitterly cold since all her clothes were torn — poor, delicate little Thumbelina was like to freeze to death. Then it began to snow and every snowflake that fell on her was like a shovelful tossed at big folks like us, for she was only thumb-sized. She wrapped herself in a dry leaf, but that had no warmth to it and she shivered with cold.

She had now come to the edge of the wood where there was a large cornfield. The corn was long since cut and only the bare, dry stubble stuck up out of the frozen ground. That itself was like a forest for her to enter and — oh — she was so cold. But then she came to the front door of a little field mouse in a hole under the stubble. This field mouse lived there, nice and cosy with a roomful of corn and a grand kitchen and larder. Poor old Thumbelina stopped by the door like a beggar child and asked for a little bit of barleycorn, for she'd had nothing to eat for the last two days.

"Oh, you poor little thing!" said the field mouse, for she was, at heart, a kindly old field mouse. "Come on inside, into my parlour, and we'll have tea together."

When she saw what a good child Thumbelina was she said, "Well — you can stay with me over the winter, but you must clean my rooms for me and tell me stories. That's what I really like." So Thumbelina did as the kind old field mouse asked and everything went along very nicely.

"Now," said the field mouse, "we're going to be having a visitor soon. My neighbour looks in every week to say hello. He's in a better way of things than I am — he's got nice big rooms and, ooh, such a fine black fur coat. He'd make a good husband for you if you play your cards right, but he doesn't see very well. You could tell him some of your nice stories — you just see." But Thumbelina didn't fancy that idea, for this neighbour was a mole.

He came by in his black fur coat. "Very rich, very learned," said the field mouse. Oh, yes, his place *was* twenty times the size of hers and he was so knowledgeable, but he couldn't do with the sun and all those pretty flowers. He derided them because he couldn't see them. Thumbelina had to sing to him and she sang "Ladybird, Ladybird, Fly Away Home" and "The Parson's in the Glebe" and he fell for her there and then because of her sweet voice, but, being a discreet fellow, he said not a word about that.

He had recently dug a long passageway through the earth from his house to theirs and he said it would be all right for Thumbelina and the field mouse to walk along it whenever they wanted. But he told them not to be frightened of the dead bird that lay in the middle of the passageway. It was a bird, all complete with wings and beak and everything, and must have died quite recently at the start of the winter and had buried itself just where the mole had dug his tunnel.

The mole carried a piece of touchwood in his mouth, for that's a bit luminous in the dark, and he went first to light their way down the murky passage. When they came to the dead bird the mole shoved his broad nose up through the earth, making a big hole to let the daylight in. There in the hollow lay a dead swallow with its beautiful wings folded into its sides and its head and feet drawn in under its feathers – the poor thing had surely died from the cold.

How sad this made Thumbelina. She was so fond of all the little birds that had sung and twittered for her through all the long summer. But the mole gave it a shove with his stubby leg and said, "Now that's all the piping we'll be getting from him. Ugh, it must be frightful to be born a little bird. Thank God that none of my children will turn out birds with their tweet-tweet-tweeting and their starving to death in the winter."

"Yes indeed," said the field mouse, "I'd expect that from a sensible man like you. What is there for birds, for all their tweeting, when winter comes? They have to starve and freeze, even if they think that's something to be proud of as well."

Thumbelina didn't say anything, but as the other two turned their backs on the bird she bent down, lifted the feathers that lay over its head to one side and kissed its closed eyes. "Perhaps this was the one who sang so sweetly for me in the summer," she thought, "bringing me so much happiness, the dear, darling creature."

The mole stopped up the hole so that the daylight couldn't get in and followed the ladies home. But that night Thumbelina couldn't sleep so she got out of bed and wove a little blanket out of hay. Then she carried it and laid it over the dead bird along with some cotton, which she'd found in the field mouse's sitting-room, which she put round the bird's sides so that it might lie warm in the cold earth.

"Farewell, you lovely little bird," said Thumbelina. "Farewell, and blessings on you for your summer songs when the trees were so green and the sun shone on us all." And she laid her head on the bird's breast only to be startled by a faint beating within — the sound of the bird's heart. It hadn't died but lay torpid, reviving in the renewed warmth.

In the autumn, the swallows fly away to warmer places, but if one of them delays then it can be overtaken with cold, falling down as if dead and lying where it falls to be covered by the cold snow.

Thumbelina was filled with fear, trembling that the bird was so big — so big and she only a thumb-size creature — but she took courage, tucked the cotton closer round the sides of the poor old swallow and fetched the mint-leaf that she used for her own coverlet and laid it over the swallow's head. Then, the next night, she crept down to see him again and he was indeed alive, but so weak that only for a moment could he hold his eyes open and see Thumbelina, standing there holding the touchwood, which was the only light she had.

"Thank you, thank you, you darling little girl," said the sick swallow. "Oh, I am warming up so nicely. I only need to get a bit stronger and I'll be able to fly off into the warm sunshine."

"Oh, no," said she, "it's dreadfully cold out there — snow and frost are everywhere — you just stay in your warm bed and I'll look after you." And she brought him water in a flower-petal and after he'd drunk it he told how he'd torn one of his wings in a thorn-bush and couldn't keep up with the other swallows as they flew way, way off to those warmer countries. He'd fallen to the ground but beyond that could remember nothing and had no idea how he'd got where he was.

All through the winter he stayed there and good little Thumbelina took care of him. As for the mole and the field mouse, they kept clear for they didn't want to have anything to do with mouldy old swallows, dead or alive.

As soon as the spring had come and the sun warmed the earth, the swallow said his farewells to Thumbelina and she opened up the hole that the mole had made up above. The sun shone down on them so brightly that the swallow asked her if she'd like to come with him — she could sit on his back and they could fly away to the gay greenwoods. But Thumbelina knew that it would upset the old field mouse if she went away.

"No, I can't do it," she said.

"Well, goodbye then, goodbye, you dear little girl," said the swallow and he flew up into the sunshine. Thumbelina watched him go with tears in her eyes, for she loved that poor old swallow.

"*Kiweet, kiweet!*" called the bird as he flew off to the gay greenwood.

Thumbelina got very sad. She wasn't allowed to go out into the warm sunshine. The corn that had been sown in the field opposite the field mouse's house grew tall, so tall that it was like a great forest to little girls who were no bigger than a person's thumb.

"Now," said the field mouse, "with the summer coming we must work on your trousseau." For her neighbour, that tiresome mole in his black fur coat, had engaged himself to her. "You must have both wool and linen – clothes for the drawing-room and the bedroom – when you marry Mr Mole."

Thumbelina had to turn the spindle and the field mouse hired four spiders to do more spinning and weaving, night and day. Every evening Mr Mole came visiting, always rattling on about when the summer would be over and the sun wouldn't be so damned hot ("the earth's rock hard out there, y'know"). Yes, when the summer was over he'd have his wedding with Thumbelina. But she took no pleasure in the thought of that; she just couldn't stand the tiresome fellow.

Every morning at sunrise and evening at sunset, Thumbelina went out of the front door and, as the wind parted the tops of the corn so that she could see the blue of the sky, she thought how bright and fair it all was and hoped against hope that she might see her dear, friendly swallow again. But he never came. He was long gone, flying around in the gay green woods.

And now, with autumn coming on, Thumbelina's trousseau was done.

"Four weeks to wedding-day!" said the field mouse, but Thumbelina wept and said she wasn't going to take the horrid mole.

"*Snik-snak!*" said the field mouse. "None of this obstinacy, young miss, or I'll bite you with my little white teeth! That's a fine man you've got there, y'know. Why, not even the queen herself has got such a fine black fur coat. He's got food in the kitchen and wine in the cellar – just you thank the good Lord for him!"

So the wedding day arrived. Mr Mole had already come to collect his bride and she was going to live with him deep under the earth where she would never see the sun, for he couldn't abide the thing. The poor little girl was so woebegone that the field mouse let her go up to her front door to bid a last farewell to the light of day.

"Farewell, you beautiful sun!" she said, stretching her arms up into the air and taking a little step beyond the field-mouse's house. The wheat had already been harvested and only the dry stubble was left. "Goodbye, goodbye!" she cried, embracing a little red flower with her tiny arms. "Greet the little swallow from me if you ever see him!"

"*Kiweet, kiweet!*" came a sudden voice over her head and there was the self-same swallow flying over. Thumbelina rejoiced to see him and told him how she was to have this ugly mole for a husband and live down under the earth where she'd never see the sunshine. She couldn't help weeping over the whole sad business.

"Well," said the swallow, "the cold winter's on its way and I'm off to somewhere warmer – why don't you come with me? You can sit on my back – tie yourself on with your sash – and we can fly away from that miserable mole and his gloomy rooms, way over the hills to lands where the sun shines warmer than in this chilly place – somewhere where it's always summer and blossom-time. Come on quick with me, you dear little Thumbelina – you who saved my life when I was freezing to death down there."

"Yes – yes – I will come with you," said Thumbelina and climbed straight away onto the little bird's back, put her feet by his outstretched wings, tied her sash fast to one of his strongest feathers and away they went, over forests and lakes and great mountains where the snow never melts. Thumbelina was freezing in the cold air but she crept in under the swallow's warm feathers, sticking her little head out only to watch the fleeting landscapes beneath her.

And so they arrived in a world of warmth. The sun shone more brightly than it does here; the sky seemed twice as resplendent; all among the hedges and ditches luscious green and purple grapes were ripening; orange trees and lemon trees abounded in the woods; the air was fragrant with the scent of myrtle and balsam; and little children ran around the lanes, chasing a myriad of motley butterflies. But the swallow flew further and further on and everything got more and more beautiful. Then, amid the greenery of the land and the blue of the sea, they came to an ancient palace of dazzling white marble, with vines twining their way up its tall columns.

And so they arrived in a world of warmth

Up at the top there were lots of swallows' nests and into one of these the swallow landed with Thumbelina.

"This is where I live," said the swallow, "but if you'd like to seek out one of those pretty flowers down below then I'll take you to it and you'll be just as comfy as you wish."

"Well that'll be lovely," she said, clapping her tiny hands.

There was a big white marble pillar down there which had fallen over and broken into three pieces with some nice white flowers growing in among them. The swallow flew down to it with Thumbelina and settled her on one of the broad leaves. But how astonishing! There, among the flowers, was an intzy, wintzy, dinky little man, looking as though he was made of glass, with a gold crown on his head. He wasn't much bigger than Thumbelina and had a pair of transparent wings on his shoulders. He was a flower-fairy and there was just such a dinky man-fairy or lady-fairy in every flower around them. But he was King.

"Lordy!" whispered Thumbelina to her swallow. "What a very pretty chap" – but the pretty chap was a bit frightened by the swallow, who was a whacking great giant alongside titchy little him. But then he spotted Thumbelina and cheered up no end because (as you will be expecting) she was altogether the most charming girl he ever had seen. So he took his crown off his head and put it on hers, asked her name, and said – straight off – that if she'd marry him then she could be queen over all the other flower-fairies.

Now that was certainly a better deal than being married to the son of a toad or to a mole with a black fur overcoat, so she said "yes" to the pretty prince, and all the intzy, wintzy little lady and gentlemen flower-fairies came out of their flowers, bringing presents – just like that! – and the nicest of these was a pair of transparent wings, which they'd got from a big white fly. They fixed these on to Thumbelina's back so that – bingo! – she too could flutter from flower to flower. It was all very jolly and the swallow sat up in his nest, singing his very best to them. But his heart was sorrowful for he loved Thumbelina and never wanted to be parted from her.

"We're not going to call you Thumbelina any more," said the Flower-Fairies. "It's a clumsy sort of name. We're going to call you Maia, the May-Girl."

"Bye-bye, bye-bye," said the little swallow and he flew away from the world of warmth till he got to Denmark. He had a nest there above the window where the man who likes to tell stories lives and – *kiweet, kiweet!* – that's where all this has come from.

THE LITTLE MERMAID

Far out to sea the water is blue   blue as the petals of the bluest cornflower – and it's clear – clear as the most translucent glass – oh, and it's deep, deep, deep – deeper than ever anchor plummeted – and many church-steeples would have to be piled one upon the other to reach from its bottom to its top.

And down at the bottom live the sea-people.

Now you mustn't think that there's nothing where they live but bare, white sand. Oh no, there are strange trees and plants down there, whose stalks and leaves are so flimsy that the least movement in the water makes them shift and shiver as if they were alive. And all the fishes – big ones, little ones – glide among their foliage like birds do in the upper air. In the very deepest part there stands the Sea-King's palace with walls of coral and tall pointed windows of the clearest amber. It's roofed with mussel-shells which open and close in the flow of water, all very pretty since they glint with pearls, any one of which would be a marvel if you saw it in a queen's crown.

The Sea-King down there had long been widowed, but his old mother looked after the house for him – a clever woman, so proud of her royal standing that she

wore twelve oysters in her tail while the other ladies of the court were only allowed six. What's more, she was much to be admired for her fondness for her granddaughters, the little princesses. There were six of these pretty little girls, the youngest being the most beautiful with her skin clear and soft as a rose-petal, her eyes blue as the deeps of the sea, but — just like all the others — she had no legs or feet since her body ended in a fishtail.

All the long day they could play in the castle, in the grand rooms with the waving plants growing from the walls. If the great amber windows were opened the fishes would swim in to see them just as the swallows sometimes fly in to us, but the fishes swam right up to the princesses and nibbled out of their hands and let themselves be stroked.

Just outside the palace was a great garden full of flame-red and midnight-blue plants. Sea-fruits gleamed like gold, the flowers like fire among the waving stalks and leaves. The ground itself was the finest sand but blue like burning brimstone; indeed there was a strange blue radiance over everything so that you'd think you were way up in the air with the heavens all around you rather than at the bottom of the sea. In moments of calm you could see the sun above the sea with light streaming from it as from the centre of a purple flower.

Each of the little princesses had her own small plot in the garden where she could dig and plant whatever she wanted. One modelled her little flower-bed to look like a whale, another thought that a mermaid like herself would be better, but the youngest made hers round like the sun and only put in red flowers like the sun itself. She was a strange child, quiet and thoughtful, and while her sisters decorated their plots with all sorts of strange things that had dropped down among them from sinking ships, she would just stick with those rose-red flowers like the sun, along with a handsome marble statue — a fine-looking boy, carved from pure white stone, who'd sunk to the bottom of the sea from a foundered ship. She planted round this statue a rose-red weeping-willow which grew and grew and dangled its new branches down towards the sandy floor where the shadows looked violet and moved in rhythm to the branches. To her girlish eyes, the foliage and roots seemed to be kissing each other.

She had no greater pleasure than to hear of the world of people up above. Her old grandmother had to tell everything that she knew about ships and towns, about people and animals, and she took a strange delight in hearing that up there on the earth you could smell the flowers (for that couldn't happen at the bottom of the sea) and that the trees were green and the fishes among their branches could sing so sweetly that it was a pleasure to hear them. (Those were the little song-birds that Grandma called fish, otherwise the girls wouldn't know what she was talking about since they had never seen a bird.)

"When you're fifteen," said Grandma, "you'll be allowed to dive up to the surface, sit on the rocks in the moonlight and watch the great ships go sailing by. Why — you'll see the woodlands and the towns as well."

Next year, the first of the sisters came to be fifteen, so that — since each of them was a year younger than the next — the youngest still had a whole five years to wait before she could come up from the seabed and see what the likes of ourselves were up to. But the eldest promised the others that she'd tell them what she'd seen and what she'd liked best on her first day. Grandma hadn't told them nearly enough — there was so much that they wanted to know.

None of them had such longing to hear about these things as the youngest, the quiet, thoughtful one who still had five years to wait. Many a night she would stand by the open window, looking up through the dark blue water at the fish with their flickering fins and tails. She could see the moon and stars as well. True, they looked faint and pale, but bigger than they do for us because of the water. When a black shadow passed over she reckoned it to be a whale swimming above her or a ship full of people. Little did they know that far below their keel a pretty little mermaid was stretching up towards them with her white hands.

So now the eldest princess came to be fifteen and dared the journey to the surface of the sea.

When she got back she had a hundred tales to tell, but the best thing of all, she said, was to lie on a sandbank in the quiet sea and to watch by moonlight the great town on the nearby shore with its lights glittering like hundreds of stars, to hear music and the racket and clamour of people and traders, to see the church towers with their steeples, and to hear the bells ringing. Knowing, as she did, that she could not be a part of all that only made her long for it all the more.

Ah, how the youngest sister listened to all this and then, later on, stood by the open window and looked up once more through the dark blue water, thinking of the great town with all its bustle and noise, and it seemed to her that she could hear the church bells ringing down to her under the sea.

A year later, the next sister was allowed to swim up through the sea and go off as she pleased. She dove up just as the sun was setting, the moment of her journey that she found the most glorious. The heavens seemed all gold, she said, and as for the clouds — oh, their beauty was beyond description, sailing red and violet above her! Yet faster than them, however, was a skein of wild swans flying over the water like a long white ribbon into the setting sun. She swam towards it, but as it sank the rosy glow vanished from the clouds and from the face of the sea.

A year later, it was the third sister's turn. She was the most daring of all of them and she swam up a broad river that ran into the sea. There she saw beautiful green hills lined with vineyards. She could glimpse castles and great houses amidst the spreading woodlands and hear how all the birds sang, while the sun shone with such warmth that she had to plunge under the water to cool her burning face. In a little bay she encountered a whole lot of people-children, running about, quite naked, and splashing around in the water. She wanted to play with them but they were scared and ran off, and then a little black creature — a dog — came up (she'd never seen anything like that before) and frightened her so much with its barking that she fled back to the open sea. But she never forgot all those beautiful woods and the green hills, and those pretty little children who could swim in the water even though they had never a fishtail among them.

The fourth sister had none of that daring. She stayed out in the midst of the wild sea and told them how grand it was to look across the spreading ocean with the sky above like a huge glass bell-jar. You could see ships, but so far off that they looked like seagulls. The comical dolphins turned somersaults, and the whales spouted water out of their blow-holes so that you'd think you were surrounded by fountains.

And now it was the turn of the fifth sister. Her birthday was in the winter, so her first sight of things was very different from the others'. The ocean had turned green and all around floated great icebergs, which she said were pearly to look at and far taller than the church towers built by men. They took on the strangest shapes and glittered like diamonds. She'd settled herself on one of the biggest, which panicked some mariners under sail who passed by where she was sitting with her hair streaming in the wind. But towards evening, clouds came up to cover the sky. Lightning flashed; thunder rolled; the huge blocks of ice were lifted high above the black sea, shining in the red glare. Sails were reefed on all the ships amid fear and anguish, but she sat peaceably on her floating berg, watching the blue zigzag flashes slashing into the shining sea.

When each of the sisters first found freedom in the great waters, everything seemed new and wonderful. But now that they were grown girls, free to go wherever they wished, they grew indifferent, took on a liking for where they belonged, and after a month or so had gone by they each said that things were much nicer down below — you really felt comfier at home.

On many an evening, the five sisters would link their arms and dive up to the surface all in a row. They had beautiful voices, sweeter than anything you'd find among mortals, and when a storm was on its way and they reckoned ships might go down they would swim beyond their prows, singing of the delights of the seabed and urging the sailors not to fear coming among them. But the sailors couldn't understand such words, thinking it was the sound of the storm, and they would hardly see much of the promised delights if their ship sank, as they would drown and only turn up as corpses to the Sea-King's palace.

When these sisters, arm in arm, rose through the water, their youngest sister was left quite alone watching them, and she would have wept except that mermaids have no tears to shed and that only increased her sorrow. "Oh, if only I were fifteen," she said. "I know how much I will love the world up there and all those people going about their everyday lives."

And then, at last, she was fifteen years old.

"Now we're getting you off our hands," said her grandma, the old dowager, "come and let me make you ready like your sisters." And she placed a garland of white lilies in her hair with half a pearl in each petal of the flowers, and let eight big oysters attach themselves to the princess's tail to show what a royal personage she was.

"Ow, that hurts!" said the little mermaid.

"Oh yes," said the old woman. "You've got to suffer a bit — *noblesse oblige*, y'know."

Oh, the little mermaid would have been glad enough to get rid of all this pomp and set aside the clumsy garland — the red sea-flowers would have suited her better — but there was nothing she could do about it. "Goodbye then," she cried and rose, light and pure as a bubble, up through the water.

The sun was just going down when she raised her head out of the sea, but the clouds still glowed in pink and gold, and the evening star shone bright and beautiful in the paling rose of the sky. The air was calm and fresh and the sea unmoving. A great ship with three masts lay before her, its single sail barely stirring, and sailors were lounging all around in the rigging and the yards. There was music and singing and as darkness fell they lit lanterns of all kinds – hundreds of them – and they swung about like the flags of all nations. The little mermaid swam along to the cabin window and as she rose in the swell she could see through the clear glass panes where a crowd of smartly dressed young fellows were standing. And the smartest of all, with great dark eyes, was the young prince, round about sixteen years old – and indeed, this day was his birthday which was cause for all the celebrations. The mariners danced on the decks and, when the young prince came out, more than a hundred rockets shot up into the sky, turning it back to daylight. Well, that really frightened the little mermaid and she ducked quick under the water. But she soon raised her head out again and it was as though all the stars in the heavens were falling around her. How could she ever have imagined such fireworks! Great suns whirled around – brilliant firefishes flew up into the blue night – everything was mirrored in the clear, still sea. The ship itself was so lit up that you could see every bit of rope, to say nothing of the crew. Oh, how very handsome that young prince was, shaking hands with everyone, smiling, as the music rang out through the beautiful night.

It got late, but the little mermaid could not take her eyes off the ship and the handsome prince. The lamps and lanterns were put out, no more rockets flew into the sky, the cannons fell silent and deep down in the sea there was a murmuring and a rumbling. She stayed in the water as it rose and fell, letting her see inside the cabin. But the ship moved ahead more strongly, one sail after another was spread, the waves now strengthened, great clouds rose up and there was distant lightning. Oh – a dreadful storm was in the offing. The sailors took in sail and the great ship ploughed a wild course through the wild sea. The water turned itself into huge black mountains threatening to overwhelm the masts, but the ship plunged like a swan amid the high waves and then allowed itself to be lifted again to their summits.

This seemed, to the little mermaid, to be a jolly journey, but it was by no means so to the sailors. The ship creaked and cracked, its thick planks groaned under the fearful battering, the sea rushed in, the mainmast snapped in two as though it were no stronger than a reed, and the ship heeled over on to its side as the water flooded into the hold. Now the little mermaid realised that she too was in danger and had to watch out as the ship's beams and tackle tumbled about in the water. One minute it was so pitch dark that she couldn't see the least thing, the next there was such a flash of lightning that she could see everyone on the boat, struggling as best they could. She looked out especially for the young prince and, as the ship broke up, she saw him sink into the deep, deep sea.

For a moment she rejoiced, for now he would come down to her, but then she remembered that people could not survive under water and that, dead, there would be no place for him in her father's palace. No – there was going to be no dying for him – and she swam through all the timbers and planks that flung themselves about in the sea, careless that any one of them might have smashed into her. Diving deep under the waves and then surfacing again, she finally reached the young prince who could barely swim any longer in the raging sea. His arms and legs were failing, his beautiful eyes were closed and he would surely have died if the little mermaid had not got to him. She raised his head out of the water and let the waves carry them wheresoever they chose.

By dawn the foul weather had passed, but not a trace of the ship was to be seen. The sun rose, shining red over the water, seeming to bring back life to the prince's cheeks, although his eyes stayed closed. The mermaid kissed his noble brow and stroked back his wet hair. He looked to her like the marble statue down in her little garden and she kissed him again, hoping that he would live.

And now, in front of her, there was dry land. There were high blue mountains whose tops were scattered with snow, lying there like white swans. Nearer to the seashore there were beautiful green woods and some sort of building – she'd no idea if it was a church or a convent. Orange trees and lemon trees grew in its garden and there were tall palm trees at its entrance. The sea edged into a little bay here and was dead calm but very deep. It skirted some cliffs, below which a beach of fine white sand was spread. Here it was that she swam with her beautiful prince, laying him down in the sand and taking care that his head lay above the tideline in the bright sunshine.

Bells now began to sound in the big white building and a lot of young girls came through the garden. The little mermaid therefore swam further off, between some tall rocks that rose above the water, and there she covered her hair and breast with sea-froth so that no one should see her little face. And there she waited to see who might come to find her poor prince.

She didn't have to wait long before a young girl came along. She was startled for a moment by what she saw, but then called over more people. And the mermaid saw that the prince had come to himself and was smiling at everyone around him. But he never looked over and smiled at her, for he had no idea that it was she who had saved him. This saddened her, and when they had taken him into the great building she dived sorrowfully below the surface of the sea, back to her father's palace.

She had always been the quiet, thoughtful one, and now she was more so. Her sisters asked her to say what she had seen on her first journey to the surface, but she told them nothing.

Many a morning and evening she would swim up to where she'd left the prince. She watched the fruits of the garden ripen and be garnered, she saw the snows melting on the high hills, but the prince she did not see and so always returned sorrowfully home. Her only comfort was to sit in her own little garden with her arms round the beautiful marble statue that so resembled her prince, but she did not look after her plants and they made a wilderness of the paths and tangled their leaves and stalks among the branches of the sea-trees, so that the place became very gloomy.

Eventually she could bear it no longer and told her tale to one of her sisters. That way it quickly reached the others, but no one else knew — apart from one or two other mermaids who told one or two others, in the strictest confidence of course. One of these well knew who the prince was for she too had seen the shipwreck and, what's more, she knew where he came from and where to find his kingdom.

"Come on then, little sister," said the other princesses, and with their arms round each others' shoulders they carried her up in a long line to where they knew the prince's palace to be.

This was built of a sort of pale yellow stone and had great staircases, one of which came down to the sea. Splendid gilded cupolas towered over its roofs, and marble statues, looking as though they were alive, stood between the columns that surrounded the whole building. If you could look through the clear glass of the high windows, you'd see grand rooms hung with costly silks and tapestries, every wall displaying paintings that were a delight to the eye. In the middle of the largest hall a fountain was playing, its water jetting up to the glass dome in the ceiling where

He would surely have died if the little mermaid had not got to him

the sun shone down on the plants that ornamented its basin.

So now she had seen where he lived and on many an evening, or at night, she would come there, swimming closer in than any of the others would have dared — indeed, she went right up the small inlet that ran below a big marble balcony that cast its shadow over the water. Here she sat below the young prince, who thought himself to be quite alone in the bright moonlight.

Many an evening she saw him sailing his royal boat with music playing and banners flying. She peeped at him from the green reeds, and if anyone saw her silver-white veil blowing in the wind they thought it was a swan lifting its wings.

And many a night when the boatmen were out at sea, fishing by torchlight, she would hear them singing the prince's praises, and she rejoiced that she had saved his life when he was half-dead among the waves, and she remembered how his head had lain on her breast and how passionately she had kissed him. He, though, knew nothing about all that and couldn't even dream about her.

More and more she came to love the people that she saw; more and more she desired to rise up and join them, they whose world seemed so much larger than hers. Why — they could cross the seas in ships, climb the high hills right above the clouds, and their lands, with their fields and forests, stretched further than her eyes could reach. She wanted to know so much, but her sisters didn't know enough to help, so she went and asked her old grandma who knew a good deal more about the upper earth which she rightly called, "the land above the sea".

"If people don't drown," asked the little mermaid, "can they live forever — not dying like us down here in the sea?"

"Oh yes," said the old lady, "but they can die all right and their lives are quite a bit shorter than ours. We can go on for three-hundred years but when things come to an end here we don't get anything like a grave alongside our nearest and dearest but turn into foam on the waters. There's nothing for us like an immortal soul, oh no, no life beyond for us. We're like the green rushes — no flourishing again once we're cut down. People, though, have a soul, a soul that lives forever after their bodies turn to dust. It rises up through the clear air, up to the shining stars! Just as we dive up to the top of the sea and look at the lands where people live, so they rise up to some unknown, blessed place that we shall never see."

"Why don't we get an immortal soul?" asked the little mermaid with some sorrow.

"I'd swap my hundreds of years just to be human for a day and then have some part in that heavenly world."

"Don't you ever think that," said the old lady, "we're a lot happier and better than the people up there."

"What do you mean? I shall have to die and turn into foam on the waters and never again hear the music of the waves or see the pretty sea-blossoms and the golden sun! Can't I do anything to get an immortal soul?"

"No," said the old lady, "only if a man had such love for you that you were more to him than father or mother, only if you consumed his thoughts and his love so that he had the priest lay his right hand in yours as he promised eternal faithfulness, only then would his soul pass into your body and you partake of mankind's joy. You would enter into and receive a part of his soul. But you can't do it! The thing that delights us so much here, down in the water, your fishtail, would be hateful to him up there on earth. It's not something anyone there understands. To be beautiful up there you've got to have two great clumsy supports to hold you up – legs they call them."

That made the little mermaid sigh, and she looked mournfully at her tail.

"Come on, let's be happy," said Grandma, "we've got three-hundred years of whirling around and cavorting, that's quite long enough before we enjoy a nice rest at the end of it all. Come on – this evening – let's have a court-ball!"

And that had a splendour that you'd never see on earth. The walls and ceiling of the great ballroom were made of thick, clear glass. Several hundred colossal conch-shells, rose-red and grass-green, were lined up all round, burning with a blue fire which lit up the whole room so that the sea beyond the walls was lit up too. You could see countless fish, big and small, swimming towards the glass walls, some with scales shining all purple, others gold and silver.

Through the middle of the ballroom there was a broadly flowing current where the mermen and mermaids did their dancing, singing their own peculiar music. (I'm sure you'd never hear such charming voices among people on earth.) The little mermaid was the most beautiful singer of them all and they clapped their hands for her – a moment of joy which went to her heart, for she realised that she had the loveliest voice of anyone, either in the sea or on land.

But that brought her to think again of the earth above, and she could not forget the handsome prince or that, unlike him, she had no immortal soul. So she crept out of her father's palace with all its music and pleasure and went sadly to her little garden. There she heard a horn sounding through the water and she thought, "Now he is sailing up there, he whom I love more than father or mother, he on whom all my thoughts are fixed and in whose hand I will lay my life's happiness. I will dare everything to gain him and his immortal soul. While my sisters are dancing away in my father's palace, I will go to the Sea-Witch. She has always terrified me, but perhaps she can advise or help me now."

So the little mermaid set out from her garden for the roaring whirlpools behind which the Sea-Witch lived. She had never before taken that way, where never a flower bloomed amongst the seaweed and only bare grey sand spread out towards the maelstroms where the water whirled round like a roaring millwheel, hurling everything caught up in it down to the oceanic deeps. She had to go through these roiling whirlpools to get to the Sea-Witch's domain and then for a long stretch there was no other way except across warm, bubbling mud, which the witch called her peatbog.

Behind it lay her house in a peculiar wood. All the trees and bushes in it were polypes: half animal, half plant, looking like hundred-headed snakes growing out of the ground. All their branches had long, slimy arms with fingers like elastic worms that slithered about, joint by joint, from their roots to their very tips. Everything that they could grasp in the water they seized, never again to let it go. Standing in front of them the little mermaid was terrified, her heart beat with fear and she was ready to turn back, but she thought of the prince and the soul of man, and that gave her courage. She bound her loose, flyaway hair tight to her head so that the polypes would not seize it, placed both hands over her breasts and skimmed through the water the way fish do, past the hateful polypes which stretched their flexile arms and fingers after her. She saw that every one of them held something that it had caught, hundreds of little arms tenacious as iron bands. You could see bundles of white bones wrapped in those arms that were all that was left of men who had drowned. They held fast to ships' rudders and chests, the skeletons of animals, and even a little mermaid whom they'd trapped and strangled. As you may guess, that terrified her the most.

Now she had reached a big, marshy place in the woodland where great fat water-snakes gambolled, showing their ugly, whitish-yellowish bellies. In the middle of this bog a house had been built from the whitened bones of drowned men. There sat the Sea-Witch feeding a toad out of her own mouth in the way that some people let canary birds take sugar. She called the foul watersnakes "my little chickens" and let them crawl around her great spongy breast.

"I know what you want, you stupid girl," said the Sea-Witch. "Oh yes, you can have your way, my pretty little princess, for all that it will bring you grief. You want to do away with your fishtail and have those stumps that let you walk like a man, just so that young prince will fall for you and you'll get him along with his immortal soul!" And the witch laughed so loudly and nastily that the toads and the snakes fell off her and grubbed about on the ground.

"Well, you've come just at the right time," said the witch. "If you'd come after sunrise tomorrow I wouldn't have been able to help you for another year. I'll make a concoction for you and, before sunrise, you must swim to the land, sit yourself down on the beach and swallow it all. Then your tail will split and shrink and you'll get what people call 'nice legs'. But it's going to hurt. Like a sharp sword going through you. Everyone who sees you is going to say you're the most beautiful young thing they've ever seen. Oh, you'll walk so gracefully — never a dancer so graceful as you — but every step you take will be like stepping on a knife sharp enough to make you bleed. If you really wish to suffer all that, then I'm the one to help you."

"Yes," said the little mermaid, with her voice trembling, and she thought of the prince and how she might come by an immortal soul.

"But just think on," said the Sea-Witch, "once you get to be like people you can never get back to being a mermaid, never again swoop down through the water to your sisters and to your father's palace. And if you don't win that prince's love so that he forgets his father and mother, thinks only of you, and has the priest join your hands each to the other, so that you become his wife and his queen — if that doesn't happen — then, whoosh, no immortal soul for you, and the first morning after he is pledged to someone else your heart will break and you'll turn to foam on the sea's face."

"I'll do it," said the little mermaid, though she was pale as death.

"Well, you'll have to pay me," said the Sea-Witch, "and my price is Suffering. You know very well that you've got the most beautiful voice of everyone down here below the sea and I know very well that you're after using it to get him, but you must give that voice to me. I'll have the best of you for this very expensive potion

of mine. Why, there'll be some of my own blood in it — sharp as a two-edged sword the stuff will be."

"But if you take away my voice," said the little mermaid, "what is there left for me?"

"Oh," said the witch, "you'll see — a beautiful body, a fetching walk, your come-hither eyes, they'll break a few hearts. Come on now, if you've got the guts? Stick out your little tongue so that I can cut it out by way of payment and I'll brew the magic stuff."

"Go on then," said the little mermaid, and the witch got out her stew-pot to make the potion. "Cleanliness is next to godliness," she said and scoured out the pot with some of the snakes that she'd knotted up into a bundle. Then she made a cut in her breast and let some of her black blood drip into it. Steam came out in twisting waves, enough to scare you to death, with the witch throwing various things into the pot every now and then, and as it cooked through there was a sound like weeping crocodiles. Then it was done and it looked like purest water.

"There you are then," said the witch and cut out the little mermaid's tongue so that she was dumb, never more either to speak or sing.

"If those polypes want to grab you when you go through my wood," said the witch, "then just flick a drop of the potion at them and all those arms and fingers will fly into smithereens!" But the little mermaid had no need of that for when the polypes saw the glimmering potion, shining in her hand like a twinkling star, they pulled back in terror. And so she returned through the wood and the bog and the whirling maelstrom.

She could see her father's palace. The torches had been put out in the great ball-room. Everyone slept, but she did not dare to venture among them now that she was dumb and was leaving them forever. It seemed as though her heart was breaking with sorrow and she crept into the garden, took a flower from each of her sisters' flower-beds, blew a thousand kisses to the palace, and made her way up through the dark blue waters of the sea.

The sun had not yet risen when she got to the prince's palace and climbed the splendid marble staircase. There was a radiant moon. The little mermaid drank the fierce, burning potion and it was as though a double-edged sword sliced through her body. She fainted and lay as though dead.

It was the sun shining over the sea that brought her to, smarting with pain, but

Steam came out in twisting waves, enough to scare you to death

there, standing before her and looking at her with his coal-black eyes, was the handsome young prince. She looked down and saw that her fishtail was gone and that she had the slimmest and most shapely white legs that ever a young girl might have. She was, though, quite naked and so sought to cover herself with the long tresses of her hair.

The prince asked her who she was, and how she came to be there, and she looked at him with her gentle mournful, dark-blue eyes, but not a word could she say. So he took her by the hand and led her up to his palace. As the witch had predicted, every step that she took was like treading on pointed needles or sharp knives, but she suffered it gladly and, holding the prince's hand, she walked light as a soap-bubble so that both the prince and everyone else marvelled at the grace of her movements.

She was dressed in rich silks and muslins, the most beautiful girl in the palace, but she was dumb and could neither speak nor sing. Lovely slave girls dressed in gilded silks stepped forward and sang for the prince and his royal kin and the prince clapped his hands and smiled at one who sang more beautifully than all the others. But the little mermaid knew that she herself would have far outdone her and she thought, "Oh, he cannot know that, for his sake, I have surrendered my voice forever!"

Then the slave-girls danced with graceful, swaying bodies to captivating music and the little mermaid raised her beautiful white arms and, balancing on her toes, danced across the floor with a charm beyond what had ever been seen before. Every gesture revealed her beauty more clearly, every glance touched the heart far more deeply than all that slave-girl music.

Everyone was in raptures about her, especially the prince who called her his "little foundling girl". She danced continually even though every time her feet touched the ground those sharp knives seemed to cut into them. The prince said that she should always be with him and allowed her to sleep at his door on velvet pillows.

He had a suit of a companion of the royal household made for her so that she could go with him on horseback. They would ride through the springtime woodlands with the green branches sweeping their shoulders and the little birds singing from the fresh new foliage. She climbed with the prince into the high hills, and although her delicate feet bled for all to see she laughed it off and followed him up till the clouds lay below them like a flock of birds flying to distant lands.

At night, back home at the prince's palace, when everyone was asleep, she would walk down the great marble staircase to cool her burning feet in the cold sea and would think of those in the deeps below. But then, one night, her sisters came up with their linked arms, singing sorrowfully as they swam over the water. So she beckoned to them and they recognised her and told her of the woe that she had brought to everyone. And so it was that they would come to see her every night, and indeed, one night, she saw her old grandmother who hadn't come up to the surface for many a long year, and there too was the Sea-King with his crown on his head, stretching his hands towards her – but they dared not come as close to the shore as her sisters.

Day by day the prince became more and more fond of her, seeing her as a dearly loved, good child, but with never a thought that she might be his queen. And that she had to be in order to gain her immortal soul or else, if he wedded another, dissolve into the foam of the sea.

"Do you not treasure me beyond all others?" her eyes seemed to say when he took her in his arms and kissed her innocent forehead.

"Ah, yes," said the prince, "you are most dear to me, the best-hearted of all and surely the most devoted, and you remind me of a young girl I once saw, but never expect to find again. I had been in a shipwreck and was thrown ashore near a sort of temple where several young girls were at worship. The youngest of them found me on the beach and saved my life and though I only saw her twice she is the only person in the world I would choose to marry. But you are so like her, driving her image from my soul – she is out there, in her holy temple, and fortune has sent you to me instead. We must never part."

"Oh!", sighed the little mermaid, "he has no idea that it was I who saved his life. I was the one who carried him through the sea to that woodland bay where the temple stands. I was the one who sat among the breakers afterwards to see if anyone should come. I saw that pretty girl that he loves more than me." And the little mermaid sighed deeply, for she could not weep. "Well, he's said that the girl belongs to the temple and will not come out into the world – they'll meet no more. But I am with him; I see him every day; I will cherish him, love him, lay down my life for him."

Now it was time for the prince to marry and people said that he ought to have the beautiful daughter of a next-door king, and they fitted out a splendid ship to get matters underway. The idea was that this would be a state visit to the kingdom, but it was really done so that he could get a good look at the king's daughter. He was to have a large retinue, but the little mermaid shook her head and smiled, for she knew more about the prince's thoughts than anyone else. "I've got to go there," he said, "my parents want me to see this beautiful princess, but they're not compelling me to bring her back here as a royal bride. I really can't love her! She'll have nothing on that pretty girl at the temple that looked like you. If it's up to me to choose a bride then I'd sooner choose you, my dear dumb foster child, with your wise eyes!" and he kissed her red lips, stroked her long tresses, and laid his head upon her heart so that she dreamed of gaining human love and an immortal soul.

"You're not afraid of the sea then, my dumb child," he said when they stood by the splendid ship that was to ferry them to the land of the next-door king. And he told her a lot about storms and calm seas, of strange fish that lived in the deeps and what divers had found there, and she smiled at his stories for she knew better than anyone what went on at the bottom of the sea.

That moonlit night, when everyone slept except for the steersman standing at the helm, she sat on the ship's gunwale and gazed through the clear water, seeming to see her father's palace with her old grandmother on its battlements, with her silver crown on her head gazing back up at the ship's keel through the streaming water. And then her sisters dove up to the surface looking at her sorrowfully and wringing their white hands. She beckoned to them, smiled, and would like to have shown them how well and happy she was, but the ship's boy came up to her just then and her sisters dived down so that he thought the whiteness that he saw was just foam on the sea.

The next morning, the ship sailed into the harbour of the next-door king's magnificent city. The church bells were all ringing and trumpets sounded from high towers while soldiers stood with waving banners and glinting bayonets. There was feasting every day. Balls and parties followed one after another, but the princess wasn't there yet. People said that she had to come from a holy temple far away where she'd been schooled in royal virtues. Then, eventually, she arrived.

The little mermaid was very desirous of seeing just how beautiful was this princess and she had to admit that she'd never seen so lovely a creature. Her skin was radiantly pure and behind her long, dark eyelashes smiled a pair of steady, dark-blue eyes.

"It's you!", cried the prince, "you who saved me when I lay like a done-for corpse on that lonely shore!" and he drew this bride, covered in blushes, into his arms. "Oh," he said to the little mermaid, "what joy! The best that I ever dared hope for has come to me. You will rejoice in my happiness, you, who are closer to me than anyone!" And the little mermaid kissed his hand and felt that her heart was breaking. The morning of his wedding would bring her death, transform her to foam upon the ocean.

All the church-bells rang out and heralds rode the streets announcing the betrothal. Scented oil was burned in silver vessels on all the altars, priests swung their censers, and the bride and bridegroom joined hands to receive the bishop's blessing. The little mermaid, dressed in silk and gold, bore the bride's train, but her ears heard none of the festal music, her eyes did not see the holy ceremony, she thought only of this as the night of her death and of all she had lost in the world.

That same evening the bride and bridegroom went on board the ship. Cannons roared, flags waved, and amidships there was raised a royal tent of gold and purple, and there the bridal pair, cushioned in luxury, were to spend the still, cool night.

The sails swelled with the wind and the ship, barely rocking, glided out over the clear sea.

As darkness fell, a host of lamps were lit and the crew on deck danced jolly sailor dances. The little mermaid could not help but think of that first time when she had come up through the sea and watched the same joy and splendour, and she whirled herself into the dancing, swerving and dipping as a swallow swerves when it is chased, and everyone marvelled, filled with admiration, for she had never danced so wonderfully before. Those sharp knives cut away at her tender feet, but she could not feel them for the agony in her heart. She knew this would be the last evening when she would see him, he for whom she had given up family and home, surrendered her sweet voice, and suffered endless pain each day of which he knew nothing at all. This would be the last evening when she would breathe the same air as he breathed, and see the deeps of the sea and the star-studded sky. An eternal night awaited her, without thoughts or dreams, for she had no soul nor yet now might gain one. And the partying on the ship went on till after midnight and she laughed and danced with death in her heart. The prince kissed his delectable bride, and she stroked his dark hair and then, arm in arm, they went to their rest in the magnificent tent.

The ship now became quiet and still. Only the steersman remained standing at the helm, and the little mermaid laid her arm again along the gunwale and looked eastward towards the dawn, where the first glimpse of the rising sun would kill her. And then she saw her sisters rising out of the water, pale as she was herself, their beautiful long hair no longer swirling about their shoulders for they had been shorn.

"We have given it to the witch so that this night she might help us to save you from dying. She has given us this knife — look, here it is — see how sharp it is! What you must do, before the day dawns, is stab it into your prince's heart and as his warm blood is spattered over your feet they will grow back into a fishtail and you'll become a mermaid again. You can come back to us in the water and have your three-hundred years before you die and turn into foam in the salt sea. Hurry! Either you or he has got to die before sunrise! Our old granny is so wretched that she is losing her white hair, just as ours fell from the witch's scissors. Stab that prince — come back to us — look, look, there's already a glow in the heavens — the sun will be up any minute — you'll die!" and with a strange, deep, moaning sigh they sank beneath the waves.

The little mermaid drew back the purple curtaining of the tent and saw the lovely bride sleeping with her head on the prince's breast. She bent and kissed him on his untroubled forehead. She looked at the dawn-light increasing more and more, she looked at the whetted knife and then turned her eyes again on the prince, murmuring his bride's name in his dreams, for only she was in his thoughts. The knife trembled in the little mermaid's hand — but then she hurled it far out into the waves where it shone red as it fell and it seemed to be dripping drops of blood into the water. Once more she gave a heartbroken glance to the prince and, flinging herself from the ship into the water, felt her body dissolving into foam.

AN EPILOGUE

Thus was the curse of the Sea-Witch fulfilled. But either the curator of immortal souls or he from whom this story came took pity on the little mermaid, for whom so many difficulties had been contrived, and our sources tell us that the intervention of some Higher Power served, as we now see, to mitigate her final dissolution:

As the sun rose out of the sea its beams fell with a comforting warmth on the deathly cold sea-foam and the little mermaid did not feel the touch of death. She looked into the bright sun and saw, swirling above her, hundreds of graceful, diaphanous creatures. Through them she could see the white sails of the ship and the rosy clouds in the sky. There was melody in their voices but so ethereal that no human ear could hear it, just as no earthly eye could see them. Wingless, they swirled through the ether with a lightness all their own, and the little mermaid saw that she too had a form like theirs, rising out of the foam.

"Where am I going?" she cried, and her voice rang out like those of the other beings, so ethereal that no earthly music could equal it.

"To the daughters of air!" answered the others. "Mermaids may have no immortal soul but they may create one without seeking the love of a mortal. Their eternal life may depend on a strange power. The daughters of air themselves have no eternal soul, but they may create one through pure goodness. Thus, we may fly to tropic lands where people are killed by the pestilential heat and we bring a coolness to them — a coolness with the scent of flowers — healing and heartening. After three-hundred years of striving to do all the good we can, we gain an immortal soul and enter into the eternal joy of mankind. Ah, you poor little mermaid, you too have striven, like us, with your whole heart; you have suffered and endured, raising yourself to the world of the Spirits of the Air. Now you too may, through three-hundred years of kindnesses, create for yourself an immortal soul." So the little mermaid raised her shining arms towards God's sun and for the first time felt the fall of her own tears.

On the ship, bustle and noise had returned. She saw both the prince and his lovely bride looking for her and gazing woefully at the billowing foam as though they knew that she had thrown herself into the waves. Invisibly, she kissed the brow of the prince's bride, smiled at him and rose up with the children of air, up through the rose-red clouds, sailing into the ether.

"In three-hundred years we shall float thus into the Kingdom of God!"

"Ah!", whispered one, "we may get there even sooner. Invisible as we are, we may come into the houses of mortals with children and every day that we find a good child who brings happiness to his parents and deserves their love, God shortens our time of probation. Children do not see how we fly through their rooms and when we smile at their happiness then a whole year drops from our three-hundred. But if we see a naughty or spiteful child then we shed tears of grief and for every tear a day is added to our task."

THE EMPEROR'S NEW CLOTHES

Many years ago there lived an Emperor who was so very fond of beautiful new clothes that he spent all his money on being gorgeously dressed. He didn't care about his soldiers, he didn't care about the theatre or about drives in the park — except only for showing off his new clothes. He'd got a robe for every hour of the day, and just as you might say of one king or another, "He's in his council chamber," so you'd say here, "The Emperor is in his wardrobe!"

There was always a lot of jollification going on in the big city where he lived, with plenty of strangers arriving every day — and one such day a couple of swindlers turned up. They put it about that they were weavers and said that they knew how to weave the finest cloth you could think of. Not only were the colours and patterns uncommonly beautiful, but any clothes sewn from this cloth had the extraordinary property of being invisible to anyone who couldn't do his job properly or who was unforgivably stupid.

"Well those would certainly be fine clothes," thought the Emperor. "With clothes like that I could find out whoever in the empire isn't fit for office — and I'll be able to tell the wise from the stupid! Yes indeed, they must weave some of that cloth for

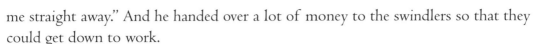

me straight away." And he handed over a lot of money to the swindlers so that they could get down to work.

So they set up two looms there and then, and pretended to work, but they had absolutely nothing in the frames. Right away they called for the finest silk and the most magnificent gold thread – and all this they put into their own bags and carried on working at the empty looms till far into the night.

"Now I should certainly like to know how far they've got along with that cloth!" thought the Emperor, but he was a bit uneasy when he came to think that no one who was stupid, or not fit for his job, would be able to see it. (Not of course that he need worry – he was pretty confident about that!) Still, he'd better send someone else first to see how matters stood. Everyone throughout the city knew about the extraordinary powers of the cloth and everyone was eager to see how incompetent or stupid his neighbour was. "I'll send my honest old Prime Minister to the weavers," thought the Emperor, "he can best see how the cloth looks, for he's got brains and no one's better fit for office than him."

So off went the trusty old Prime Minister to the room where the two swindlers sat and worked at their empty looms. "Good heavens!" thought the old man, opening his eyes very wide. "I can't see a thing!" But he didn't say that.

Both the swindlers begged him to be so good as to step closer, and then asked if it wasn't a beautiful pattern, and weren't the colours charming? And they pointed to the empty loom, and the poor old Prime Minister kept peering as hard as he could, but he saw nothing, for there was nothing. "Good Lord," he thought, "could I possibly be stupid? I never thought I was. No one must ever know! Or could I possibly be no good at my job? No, no! It will never do for me to say that I can't see the cloth!"

"Well now," said the one who was weaving, "you're not saying anything about it!"

"Oh – it's lovely – quite wonderful!" said the old Prime Minister, and squinted through his spectacles. "This pattern! And these colours! Yes, I shall certainly tell the Emperor that it pleases me enormously."

"Ah well, we're happy to hear that," said both the weavers, and they called attention to the colours by name, and the curious design. The old Prime Minister listened carefully so that he could repeat it all when he got home to the Emperor – and that's just what he did.

Now the swindlers asked for more money and yet more silk and gold, which they needed for the weaving. They put it all into their own pockets – not a single thread

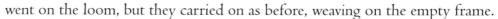

went on the loom, but they carried on as before, weaving on the empty frame.

Before long the Emperor sent yet another honest official to see how things went with the weaving and if the cloth would be ready soon. He fared no better than the Prime Minister: he looked and looked, but since there was nothing there but the empty loom, nothing could he see.

"There now! Isn't that a beautiful bit of cloth?" said both the swindlers, pointing out and describing the delicate pattern, which wasn't there at all.

"Well, I'm not stupid," thought the man, "could I really not be fit to hold my responsible position? How very curious! But of course it won't do to let anyone notice." So he praised the cloth that he couldn't see and assured them of his delight in the pretty shades and the lovely patterns. "Oh, indeed! It's absolutely wonderful!" he said to the Emperor.

Everyone in the city was talking about the marvellous cloth. So now the Emperor himself wanted to see it all, while it was still on the loom. With a whole crowd of hand-picked gentlemen (among whom were the two poor old officials who had been there before) he paid a visit to the crafty swindlers who were weaving away for all they were worth, but with never a twist of thread between them.

"Ah! Is it not *magnifique*?" said the two honest officials. "May it please your Majesty to observe... Such a design! Such colours!" And they pointed to the empty loom, sure that others could probably see the cloth.

"What's all this?" thought the Emperor. "I can't see a thing! But that's frightful! Am I not fit to be Emperor? That would be the most terrible thing that could ever happen to me! – Oh, it's very beautiful!" said the Emperor. "It has our most gracious approval!" And he nodded happily and looked at the empty loom; he wasn't going to say that he couldn't see anything. The whole retinue that he'd brought with him looked and looked, but they could make nothing more of it than anyone else – but, like the Emperor, they all said, "Oh, it's very beautiful!" and they advised him to order some clothes from this new and wonderful material to wear for the first time in the grand procession that was soon to take place. "It is *magnifique*! Delectable! *Superbe!*" went the words from mouth to mouth, and everyone was just enchanted with the whole affair. The Emperor awarded each of the swindlers the Knight's Great Cross to hang from his button-hole and gave them the title of Esquires of the Loom.

For the whole night before the morning when the procession was to take place

the two swindlers sat up with over sixteen candles burning. People could see that they were busy trying to get the Emperor's new clothes ready in time. They made out that they were taking cloth from the loom; they snipped at the air with big scissors; they sewed away with needles without any thread; and finally they said, "There! The clothes are finished!"

The Emperor, with his most distinguished gentlemen-in-waiting, arrived in person and the two swindlers each lifted one arm in the air, as if they were holding something between them and said, "Look, here are the breeches! Here's the robe! Here's the cloak!" and so forth, and so on. "It's as light as a cobweb! Indeed, one might think one had nothing on at all – but then that's just the beauty of it!"

"Quite!" answered all the gentlemen-in-waiting, but they could see nothing, for there was nothing.

"Would it please Your Imperial Majesty to remove your clothes now?" asked the swindlers. "Then we shall dress Your Majesty in the new ones over here by the large mirror!"

The Emperor took off all his clothes and the rascals pretended to hand him each piece of the new ones that they were supposed to have woven. They reached round his middle as if they were tying something on, and that was the train and the Emperor twisted and turned in front of the mirror.

"Why, how well the clothes suit Your Majesty! How well they fit!" said everyone. "What a design! What colours! That is indeed an elegant dress!"

"The canopy to be borne above Your Majesty in the procession awaits Your Majesty outside," said the Imperial-Chief-Master-of-Ceremonies.

"Yes, as you see, I'm all ready!" said the Emperor. "Doesn't it fit well?" And he made yet another turn in front of the mirror, for he wanted to look as though he was really admiring his finery.

The Chamberlains, who were supposed to carry the train, fumbled about with their hands on the floor as if they were lifting up the train. They walked off holding thin air, not daring to let anybody think that they couldn't see a thing.

And so the Emperor walked in the procession under the lovely canopy and all the people in the street and at the windows said, "Why, the Emperor's new clothes are matchless! What a beautiful train to the robes! How beautifully it fits!" For nobody wanted it thought that he couldn't see anything, because that would mean that he wasn't fit for his job or that he was stupid. Never before had the Emperor's clothes

"Why, the Emperor's new clothes are matchless!"

been such a success.

"But he hasn't got anything on!" said a little child.

"Good Lord! Listen to the voice of innocence," said his father; and everyone whispered to everyone else what the child had said.

"He hasn't got anything on – that's what the little chap was saying – he hasn't got anything on!"

"He hasn't got anything on!" shouted the whole crowd in the end. And the Emperor shivered to himself – for it seemed to him that they were right, but he thought, "Ah well, I must go on with the procession." And he carried himself yet more proudly and the Chamberlains followed, carrying the train that wasn't there at all.

THE STEADFAST TIN SOLDIER

Once upon a time there were twenty-five tin soldiers – all brothers because they were made from an old tin spoon. They shouldered their muskets, eyes to the front, very handsome in their red and black uniforms. The first thing they heard in all the world, when the lid was taken off the box where they lay, were the words "Tin soldiers!" They were shouted by a little boy, who clapped his hands, for he'd been given them for his birthday, and now he stood them up on the table. Each soldier was exactly like the rest, except for one who was a bit odd: he'd only got one leg because he'd been made last and there hadn't been enough tin to go round. Even so, he stood just as firm on his one leg as the others on their two, and he's the one who turned out to be worth talking about.

On the table, where they'd been stood up, there were lots of other toys, but the one that really caught your eye was a beautiful paper castle. You could see right into the rooms through the tiny windows, while outside tiny trees stood round a little mirror that was meant to be a lake. Swans made of wax were swimming on it and were reflected in it. It really was absolutely beautiful – but the most beautiful thing of all was a little lady who stood right in the open door of the castle. She too had been cut out of paper, but she had a skirt on, made of the finest muslin, and a narrow little blue ribbon over her shoulder like a sash — and in the middle of this there was a glittering tinsel star as big as her head. The little lady stretched out both her arms, for she was a dancer, and she lifted one leg so high in the air that the tin-soldier couldn't see where it was, so he thought that she'd only got one leg, just like him.

"That would be the wife for me," he thought, "but she's very grand. She lives there in that castle while I've only got a box and there are twenty-five of us in that so there's not much room for her! Still — we must try to get acquainted." And so he lay down full length behind a snuff box which stood on the table. Here he could easily watch the dainty little lady who went on standing on one leg without losing her balance.

When evening came, all the other tin soldiers were put back in their box and the people of the house went to bed. Now the toys began to play games: 'visiting', 'little wars', 'holding a dance'. The tin-soldiers rattled about in their box, because they wanted to join in, but they couldn't get the lid off. The nutcrackers turned somersaults and the slate-pencil played games on the slate. There was such a to-do that the canary woke up and began to talk as well — and he spoke in verse. The only two who never moved from their places were the tin soldier and the little dancer. She held herself so straight on the tips of her toes with both arms outstretched, and he was just as steadfast on his single leg. Never for a moment did he stop looking at her.

Now the clock struck twelve and — whisk! — the lid sprang up from the snuff box; but there was no tobacco in it, oh, no, just a little black goblin, for you see it was a trick snuff box.

"Tin soldier!", said the goblin, "you keep your eyes to yourself."

But the tin soldier pretended that he hadn't heard him.

"All right — you wait till tomorrow," said the goblin.

So when it was morning and the children got up, the tin soldier was stood up in the window and (either it was the goblin or the draught that did it) the window suddenly flew open and the soldier fell head-over-heels from the third floor. That was a terrible journey — his leg stuck straight up in the air and he finished up on his helmet with his bayonet caught between the paving-stones.

The servant girl and the little boy came down straight away to look for him but, although they almost trod on him, they couldn't see him. If the tin soldier had called out, "Here I am!" then they might have found him, but he didn't consider it proper to yell like that because he was in uniform.

Now it began to rain, the drops fell thicker and faster till it was a real storm, and when it was over two street-urchins came along.

"Hey look!" said one of them. "There's a tin soldier – let's sail him!"

So they made a boat out of a newspaper, put the tin soldier in, and he sailed off down the gutter. The two boys ran beside him clapping their hands. Lord preserve us! What waves there were in the gutter and what a flood it was – but then it really had been raining. The paper boat plunged up and down and now and then spun round so quickly that the tin soldier was dizzy; but he stayed steady, never flinched, and went on shouldering his musket, eyes front.

All at once the boat floated into a long gutter-pipe – as dark as if he were back in his box.

"Where am I coming to now?" he thought. "Oh, yes, this is all the goblin's fault! Ah, but if the little lady were here in the boat I wouldn't care if it were twice as dark!"

Just then a big water-rat came along who lived in the gutter-pipe.

"Got a passport?" asked the rat. "Let's have your passport."

But the tin soldier kept quiet and held his musket tighter than ever. The boat shot past with the rat after it. Hoo! How he snapped with his teeth and shouted out at bits of straw and wood, "Stop him! Stop him! He's not paid the toll! He's not shown his passport!"

But the current got stronger and stronger. The tin soldier could already spy daylight where the pipe ended, but he also heard a roaring noise which might well have terrified a braver man than he was. Just you think about it – there, where the pipe ended, the water gushed out into a big canal and that was as dangerous for him as sailing over a waterfall would be for us.

By now he was so near it that he couldn't stop. The boat sped out and the poor tin soldier held himself as upright as he could – no one should say of him that he even blinked his eyes. The boat whirled round three... four times and then filled up to the brim with water – it had to sink. The tin soldier stood up to his neck in water and the boat sank deeper and deeper; the paper fell apart more and more and now the water came over the soldier's head – then he thought of the pretty little dancer that he'd never see again, and there sounded in the tin soldier's ears the old song:

Onward, onward, warrior-man
The time has come to die!

And the paper parted and the tin soldier fell through – but at that moment he

"Let's have your passport."

was swallowed by a great big fish.

My word – but it was dark in there! It was even worse than in the gutter-pipe, and it was also very tight – but the tin soldier was steadfast and lay there, full-length, with his musket on his shoulder.

The fish jumped about, making the most amazing twists and turns, till at last he was still and something flashed through him like lightning. Daylight shone clear and someone cried out loud, "A tin soldier!"

The fish had been caught, taken to market, sold and brought up to the kitchen where the cook cut him open with a large knife. She seized the soldier round his middle with two fingers and carried him off to the room where everyone wanted to see this remarkable man who'd travelled about inside a fish – but the tin soldier didn't let it go to his head. They stood him up on the table and there – whoever would believe such wonders in the world! – the tin soldier was in the self-same room that he'd been in before.

He saw the self-same boys, and the same playthings were on the table: the beautiful castle with the pretty little dancer. She still balanced herself on one leg and held the other high in the air, for she too was steadfast. That moved the tin soldier. He almost wept tin tears, but that wouldn't have been proper. He looked at her, and she looked at him, but they never said a word.

Then all of a sudden one of the small boys took the soldier and threw him straight into the stove – without any reason whatsoever. No doubt the goblin in the snuff box was really to blame.

The tin soldier stood there brilliantly lit, and felt a terrible burning – but he didn't know if that was because of the actual fire or because of his love. All his colours were gone, but no one could tell if that was because of his journeyings or because of grief. He looked at the little lady, she looked at him, and he felt himself melting, but he still stood there steadfast with his musket on his shoulder. Then the door opened. The draught picked up the dancer and she flew like one of the sylphides straight to the tin soldier in the stove, burst into flames and was gone. Then the tin-soldier melted down into a lump and when the cook came next day to take the ashes out she found him like a little tin heart. All that was left of the dancer was the tinsel star and that was burned black as coal.

The Wild Swans

Far away from here, where the swallows fly when winter comes, there lived a king who had eleven sons and one daughter: Elise. The eleven brothers, all of them princes, went to school with stars on their tunics and swords at their sides. They did their writing lessons with diamond pencils on golden slates and read out loud just as well as to themselves. You could tell straight away they were princes. Their sister, Elise, used to sit on a little stool of mirror-glass and had a picture book that cost half the kingdom.

Oh, how happy they all were — but such things do not last. Their father, who was king over the whole country, married an evil queen, who had it in for the poor children from the very first day. There was a great feast in the palace and the children were playing a game of 'visitors', but instead of giving them the usual leftover cakes and roasted apples, the queen gave them a teacup full of sand and said they could pretend it was something nice.

A week later she sent little Elise off to live with some peasants in the country and, not long after, she told the king such make-believe stories about the poor princes that he stopped caring about them.

"Fly off into the world and look after yourselves," said the wicked queen. "Fly off like great voiceless birds!" But the result wasn't as brutal as she wanted, for they turned into beautiful wild swans. With a strange cry they flew out of the palace windows, out over the parkland and the trees.

It was still early morning when they came by where their sister lay sleeping in the peasants' room. They hovered over the roof, turned their long necks all about and beat their wings, but no one heard or saw them. Off they had to go, high into the sky and out across the wide world over a great, dark forest which stretched to the edge of the sea.

Poor little Elise stood in the peasants' room playing with a green leaf, for she had no other toy, and she poked a hole in the leaf and held it up to the sun and it was as though she could see her brothers' bright eyes. And as the warm sun shone on her cheeks she thought of all their kisses.

The days passed, one much as another. When a breeze blew through the rose bushes outside the house it whispered to the roses, "Who more beautiful than you?" but the roses shook their heads and said, "Elise." And when the old woman sat at her house-door of a Sunday, reading her hymn book, the breeze would blow the pages over and say to the book, "Who more saintly than you?" but the hymn book said, "Elise." And what the roses said, and the hymn book, was pure truth.

When she was fifteen Elise had to go home. And when the queen saw how beautiful her stepdaughter was, she was filled with spite and hatred. She'd have been glad to turn her into another swan like her brothers, but that was out of the question since the king wanted to see his daughter.

Early in the morning the queen went in to the bathing chamber, all marble and decked out with soft cushions and luxurious rugs, and she brought in three toads, kissed each of them and said to the first, "When Elise comes to bathe, hunker down on the top of her head and she'll get as stupid as you," and to the second she said, "Sit on her forehead so she'll get as ugly as you and her father won't recognise her. And as for you," she whispered to the third, "weigh heavy on her heart that you may corrupt her mind and bring her pain from it." And she set the toads down in the clear water, which took on a greenish colour. Then she called Elise over, undressed her and urged her into the water.

As she settled herself there the first of the toads clambered into her hair, the

second onto her forehead, and the third onto her breast. But Elise seemed not to notice them. As she rose from the bath three poppies lay on its surface. Had the creatures not been poisonous and, what's more, kissed by a witch, they might have become red roses, but they were at least flowers of the head and the heart. Such was Elise's innocence that sorcery had no power over her.

When the wicked queen saw that, she plastered her all over with walnut juice so that she looked all dirty, smeared her beautiful face with a stinking ointment and let her soft hair hang low in greasy tangles. Beautiful Elise was unrecognisable.

So it was that when her father saw her he was appalled and said that this was no daughter of his. Only the yard-dog and the swallows knew who she was, but they had no say in the matter.

Elise wept salt tears and thought of her eleven brothers gone off she knew not where. Overcome by distress, she stole out of the palace and walked all day over the fields and fens and into the great forest. She'd no idea where she was going to and in her distress she longed for her brothers, for surely, like her, they had been cast out into the world. She determined to find them.

Soon after she had got to the forest, night came on. She had lost every trace of tracks or paths so she sat herself down on the mossy ground, said her evening prayer and leaned her head against the stump of a tree. Everywhere was silent. The air was calm, and all around in the moss and the grass hundreds of glow-worms were twinkling like a kind of green fire, so that if she so much as touched a twig the glittering insects fell around her like shooting stars.

All night long she dreamed of her brothers: children again, writing on their golden slates with their diamond pencils, looking at the picture book that cost half a kingdom. But they weren't filling the slates with noughts and crosses like they used to do, but with tales of all their brave deeds and everything they'd seen and encountered. And everything had come alive in the picture book: birds sang, people came out of the book and talked to Elise and her brothers but then jumped back in again when she turned the page, so as not to muddle up the pictures.

The sun was already high in the sky when she woke up. She couldn't actually see it because of all the tall trees with their spreading branches, but its rays came through them, making a golden gauze. The greenery had a fragrance about it and the birds almost came to sit on her shoulders. There was a splashing of water where several large springs tumbled down into a lake with a lovely sandy bottom. Really thick bushes grew all round, but in one place the deer had made an opening so Elise could get down to the water, which was so clear that if the breeze hadn't lifted the leaves and branches of the bushes, she might have thought them painted on the sand below the water. Every leaf was mirrored there, whether in shadow or touched by the sun.

As soon as she saw her own face there Elise was mortified – why, how dirty and ugly she was. But when she dipped her hand in the lake and wiped her eyes and forehead her white skin gleamed through so she took off all her clothes and bathed in the clear water. You'd never have found a king's daughter more beautiful in the whole wide world.

When she'd dressed herself again and plaited her long hair, she went up to the bubbling spring, drank from her cupped hand and then wandered deeper into the forest without knowing where she was going. She thought of her brothers and thought of the Good Lord who would not forsake her. Did He not make the wild apples grow to feed the hungry? And He brought her to just such a tree, its branches heavy with fruit, where she made her midday meal and then, after propping up the laden branches, she went into the darkest part of the forest. So great was the silence that she heard only her own footsteps, only the snapping of every twig under her feet. She saw never a bird, never a ray of sunlight piercing the overwhelming dark of the trees. Their huge trunks crowded so closely, one behind another, that it seemed like a palisade hemming her in. Oh, here was a solitude she'd never known before.

Night came. Not a single glow-worm glowed in the moss as she lay down to sleep. But then it seemed to her that the branches above her parted and the Good Lord looked down on her with gentle eyes while a crowd of little angels flitted about around His head and under His arms. When she woke in the morning she did not know if she'd dreamed it or if it had really happened.

She hadn't gone more than a few steps when she met an old woman with a basket of berries, some of which she gave to Elise. Elise asked her if she'd ever seen eleven princes riding through the forest.

"No," said the old woman, "but yesterday I did see eleven swans in the stream down there and they had golden crowns on their heads." And she led Elise a bit further on where there was a stream flowing in a little valley. Trees on its banks entwined their long, leafy branches together, and where that couldn't happen, because of the way they grew, their roots had come loose from the earth and dangled among the branches over the water.

Elise said goodbye to the old woman and followed the stream down to where it reached the wide landscape of the seashore.

All the great ocean lay before the young girl, but with never a boat nor a sail in sight. What then was to be done? She studied the millions of little stones on the shingle beach, all ground into round pebbles by the waves. Glass, ironstone, rock, everything had been tumbled and shaped by water which seemed as gentle as her own hands. "It all just rolls on and on and that's how it smoothes the rough stones, so I will just go on and on too! Thank you, tumbling waves, for the lesson. My heart tells me that one day you will bring me to my darling brothers."

On some washed-up seaweed lay eleven white swans' feathers. She made a bouquet out of them. There were drops of water there, but you couldn't tell if that was the dew or tears. It was lonely there on the shore, but she didn't feel it. Why, the eternally changing sea had more to show in an hour or two than you'd see on a lake in a year. Covered by a huge black cloud, you might hear it say, "Darkness is mine too." Then the wind would get up and the waves would turn white, or when the wind died and the clouds gleamed red the sea was like a rose-petal. Now green, now white, however calm it might be there was always a gentle movement by the beach, the water rising and falling like the breath of a sleeping child.

Just as the sun was setting, Elise saw eleven wild swans with golden crowns on their heads flying shorewards. They flew one behind the other like a long white ribbon and Elise climbed up the beach to hide behind a bush, but the swans landed near her and flapped their great white wings.

As the sun sank below the sea, the swans suddenly sloughed off their skins and there stood eleven handsome princes, Elise's brothers. She uttered a loud cry, for although they were much changed she saw that it was them, and fell into their arms calling them each by name, so that they too realised this was their little sister now grown — and grown so beautiful. Laughing and crying at the same time, they saw how cruel their stepmother had been to them all.

"So long as the sun is in the sky," said the eldest one, "we brothers must be as wild swans; when it sinks, though, we take on human form again. That means at sunset we must find somewhere to land, for if we're flying in the clouds we'd just crash down as we turn into men. We don't live here any more but in just as beautiful a place the other side of the sea. It's a long way off though and there's no place in all the wide ocean for us to land for the night apart from a single little rock halfway

They flew one behind the other like a long white ribbon

across. It's only big enough for us to stand side by side and if there's a rough sea the waves spatter all over us – but we give thanks to God all the same. We spend the night there as men, otherwise we couldn't get across to our new home, for we need two of the longest days of the year to do it. That means that we can only see our father's house once a year. We can stay for eleven days, flying over the great forest to see the palace where we were born and where our father lives, and to see the high tower of the church where our mother is buried. There are the trees and woodlands of our birthright, there the wild horses gallop over the plains as we saw them in our childhood, there the charcoal-burners sing the old songs we danced to when we were boys. It is our homeland where we grew up – and now it is here that we have found you, our darling little sister! We have just two more days here before we must cross the sea again to the beautiful land where we live, for all that it is not our own. But how can we take you with us? We've not got a ship, nor a boat…"

"Oh, how shall I be able to free you?" asked their sister.

And they talked together through almost the whole night, dozing no more than an hour.

Elise woke to the sound of swans' wings rustling over her. Her brothers were once more transformed and they flew in wide circles and then off into the distance. But the youngest stayed behind, resting his swan head in her lap while she stroked his wings, and there they were together the whole day long. Towards evening the others returned and after sunset they resumed their true forms.

"Tomorrow we must fly away from here and must stay away for a whole year, but we can't leave you like this. Do you dare to come with us? If my arm's strong enough to carry you over the forest why shouldn't we all have strong enough wings to carry you across the sea?"

"Yes – yes – take me with you," said Elise.

They spent the whole night plaiting a net out of pliable osiers and tough reeds – making it big and strong. Elise laid herself down on it and as the sun rose and her brothers were again transformed into swans they seized the net with their beaks and flew high into the heavens, carrying their darling sister who was still sleeping. The hot sun shone full on her face so that one of the swans flew immediately above her to shield her with his broad wings.

They were far from land when she awoke, believing herself still dreaming, so strange it was to be carried high in the air above the sea. Beside her she found a branch laden with ripe berries along with a bundle of succulent roots which the youngest of her brothers had collected for her. She grinned her thanks up at him, for she knew that he was the one shielding her with his wings.

They were flying so high that the first ship they saw beneath them looked like nothing but a white seagull drifting on the waves. A great mountain of a cloud was behind them, where Elise could see a gigantic shadow of herself and the eleven swans. It was a picture more splendid than anything she'd ever seen before, but as the sun climbed the sky and the cloud slid away behind them the shadowy scene vanished.

On and on they flew through the whole day, whizzing like an arrow in the air, but now that they were carrying their sister they travelled slower than was usual. Bad weather was on the way as evening came on and Elise saw with fear that, as the sun set, there was no sign of the rock, standing lonely in the ocean. She felt the swans' wings beating more powerfully and thought that, alas, because of her, they would not make it. When the sun sank they would turn back into men, fall into the sea and drown. She prayed to the Good Lord from the depths of her heart but there was no rock. The black clouds came nearer. Gusts of wind threatened a storm. The clouds loomed huge and louring like a mass of lead. There was flash after flash of lightning.

The sun stood on the sea's edge. Elise's heart shook as the swans hurtled down, for she thought they were falling, but they held to a course. The sun was half under the sea's edge when she saw the little rock beneath her, sticking up like a seal's head out of the water. The sun sank very fast, seeming like a star, and Elise's foot felt firm ground beneath her; then the sun went out like the last spark of a bit of burning paper and her brothers were around her, arm linked to arm, for there was only just room for them all. The sea crashed against the rock, the water raining down on them, the heavens were continuously alight with a flaming fire, and there was peal upon peal of thunder. But the brothers and their sister held hands together and sang hymns that brought them comfort and courage.

Dawn came, with the air pure and calm, and as soon as the sun rose the swans flew from their little island with their sister Elise. The sea was still rough and, seen from high above, the white foam on its dark green surface looked like millions of swans floating in the water.

As the sun got higher Elise saw in front of her, half swimming in the air, a landscape of mountains with fields of ice shining on their sides and, stretching in front of them, what looked like a mile-long palace with one daringly built colonnade piled behind another and, below them, palm groves and enormous flowers as big as mill-wheels. She asked if this was the land they were heading for, but the swans shook their heads for what she was seeing was the beautiful, ever-changing palace of the fairy Fata Morgana, where it was forbidden to bring humankind. And as Elise gazed at it, the mountains, forest and the palace collapsed and there stood twelve proud churches, all alike, with tall towers and pointed windows. She thought that organs were playing, but it was the sea she heard. Then, as they were nearing the churches, they turned into a whole fleet of ships sailing below her, only for her to find when she looked down that it was a sea-mist drifting over the water.

Change after change like this passed before her eyes until at last she saw the country they were really going to: beautiful blue mountains with groves of cedar, cities and palaces. Long before sunset she sat before a great cave on a mountain overgrown with a tracery of green creepers that looked like embroidered carpets.

"Now let's see what you dream about here," said her youngest brother, and he showed her to her bedchamber.

"Ah, if only I could dream how to free you all," she said, and the thought possessed her so intensely that she prayed to God for His help — yes, even while she slept. And then it seemed to her that she was flying high in the air up to the cloudy palace of Fata Morgana, and the fairy came to meet her, radiantly beautiful and yet peculiarly like the old woman who gave her berries in the forest and told her about the swans with their golden crowns.

"Your brothers can be freed," she said, "but have you got the courage and the determination to do it? You saw how the sea could wear down the shingle, though it seemed gentler than your soft hands, and yet it did so without feeling the pain that your fingers might have felt, for it has no heart and could never feel the anguish that you will have to endure. Look at this stinging nettle that is here in my hand. Many such are growing round the cave where you are sleeping, and only those and the ones that grow round the graves in the churchyard will be any use to you. Remember that. You must pull up these nettles, even if they burn your hands to blisters. You must crush them with your feet till they turn to flax, and then you must spin and weave it into eleven shirts with sleeves like chainmail. When you cast those over the backs of your eleven swans, the enchantment will be loosed. But mark this well: from the moment that you begin this work till the moment it is done with — however many years it may take — you must never speak. Say but one word and it will drive like a dagger into your brothers' hearts. Their lives depend upon your tongue. Remember that."

With that, she touched Elise's hand with the nettle, which burned like fire and the girl awoke. It was bright day and just by the spot where she had been sleeping lay the nettle from her dream. Down on her knees, she gave thanks to the Good Lord and came out of the cave to begin her work.

She seized the dreadful nettles with her soft hands and they were like fire. Blisters burned her hands and arms but she rejoiced in the pain for the sake of her darling brothers. And she crushed every nettle with her bare feet and wove the green flax.

At sunset her brothers returned and were appalled to find her struck dumb – it seemed a new curse laid on them by their wicked stepmother. But when they saw her hands they realised she was doing something for their sakes. The youngest brother wept for her and where his tears fell her blisters vanished and she felt no more pain.

She spent the night working, for she could find no rest till she might release her darling brothers. And all the next day she continued through the lonely hours while the swans were away, but never had time passed so quickly. The first of the nettle-mail shirts was finished and she started on the next.

Then the sound of a hunting horn echoed through the hills and she was consumed by fear. The sounds came nearer and she heard the yelp of dogs. Terrified, she fled into her cave, bundled up the nettles that she had gathered and crushed, and sat down on them.

At that moment, a great dog sprang out of the undergrowth, followed by another and another. They barked and barked, running about, backwards and forwards, and then it was only a few minutes before all the huntsmen gathered outside the cave. The handsomest among them was the king of that country and, stepping before Elise, he found he had never seen a more beautiful girl.

"Why, child," he said, "what on earth are you doing here?" Elise shook her head, for saying anything would cost her brothers their freedom and their lives, and she tucked her hands under her apron so that the king would not see her suffering.

"Come with me," he said. "You can't stay here and if you are as good as you are beautiful, I shall dress you in silks and velvets, crown you with gold and you shall live and reign in my finest palace," and he lifted her up on to his horse. She wept and wrung her hands but the king said, "All I want is your happiness. One day you will thank me for that," and he rode off into the hills with her sitting before him on his horse with the huntsmen following after.

By sunset the splendid royal city lay before them with its churches and its cupolas. The king led her into the palace with its great fountains splashing in marble halls and its walls and ceilings adorned with paintings. But, weeping and sorrowing, she had no eyes for such things. Peaceably though, she let the waiting-women dress her in royal robes, twine pearls into her hair and draw dainty gloves over her blistered hands.

There she stood in all her glory, so dazzling in her beauty that the court bowed before her and the king chose her for his bride. As for the archbishop though, he shook his head and muttered that this girl out of the forest was a witch who had blinded the king's eyes and his heart.

But the king would have none of this. He called for music to ring out, for the costliest of dishes to be served, for the most graceful girls to dance before them, and Elise was led through sweet-scented gardens and splendid galleries. But never a smile passed her lips or shone in her eyes. She was possessed by grief.

Thus it was that the king had a little room prepared for her where she might sleep. It was adorned with a luxurious green carpet so that it might resemble in a way the cave where she had dwelt, while on the floor was the bundle of flax she had trodden from the nettles and hanging from the ceiling was the first of the shirts she had made. One of the huntsmen had brought them along as curiosities.

"Here," said the king, "you may dream yourself back into the place where we found you. Here is the work that so preoccupied you, which may carry your thoughts back to that time amid all this splendour."

When Elise saw these things that lay so close to her heart a smile broke from her lips and colour came to her pale cheeks. Thinking of her brothers' deliverance, she kissed the king's hand and he clasped her to his heart. The church bells rang out to anticipate the wedding-feast and the beautiful dumb girl from the forest was to be queen of all the land.

The archbishop whispered evil words into the king's ear, but they did not reach his heart. The wedding took place; the archbishop himself had to place the crown on the girl's head, pressing it down wickedly hard so as to hurt her, but a greater pain pressed at her heart, thinking of her brothers, and she hardly felt it.

Dumb as she was, since a single word from her would cost her brothers their lives, there nonetheless shone from her eyes a profound love for this kindly, handsome king who sought to do all he could to make her happy. Day by day her heart drew closer to him. Oh, how she wished to share with him her suffering. But dumb she must be and dumbly seek to finish her work. Thus, every night she slid from his side and went into her little cave-room, weaving one nettle-shirt after another – but when she began the seventh she found herself with no more flax.

She knew that the nettles she needed were growing in the churchyard where she would have to pull them up – but how was she to do that? "Oh," she thought, "the pain in my fingers is nothing to that in my heart. I must dare to do it and the Good Lord will bear me up in his hands." And with fear in her heart, as though she were about some evil deed, she crept into the moonlit garden and down the long avenues and lonely streets to the churchyard. There, on one of the broadest tombstones, sat a circle of lamias, those terrible witches, who tore off their rags as though they were bathing, clawed into fresh graves with their long, skinny fingers and ate the flesh of the corpses. Elise had to pass close by them and they followed her with their wicked eyes, but she offered up a prayer, gathered the burning nettles and carried them back to the palace.

Only a single person had seen her: the archbishop – awake while others slept. Now he saw that he was right in thinking that all was not well with the queen, that she was a witch who had enchanted the king and everyone else.

In the secrecy of the confessional he told the king what he had seen and what he feared, and as the harsh words left his mouth the carved figures of the saints shook their heads as if to say, "No – it is not so – Elise is innocent!" But the archbishop thought differently and claimed that they were shaking their heads at her sinfulness.

Two great tears rolled down the king's cheeks at this and he returned home with doubt in his heart. The next night he pretended to be asleep, wakeful behind his closed eyes. He marked how Elise left their bed and every night thereafter he followed her and saw how she disappeared into the cave-room.

Day by day his frowns darkened. Elise saw this but knew not why; it frightened her and how her heart suffered too for her brothers! Salt tears fell on the royal purple, lying there like glittering diamonds so that everyone who glimpsed such regal splendour wished that they too might be queens.

Through it all, though, she went on with her work and now only one nettle-shirt remained to be done, but she had no flax left and no more nettles. One last time therefore she needed to go to the churchyard and gather a few more handfuls. She thought with anguish of that lonely walk and the hideous lamias, but her will was firm and her trust was in the Lord.

So she went. But the king and the archbishop followed, saw her unlatch the wicket-gate into the churchyard and as they got nearer there the lamias were just as Elise had seen them and the king turned away his head, believing that she, who only an hour or two ago had lain on his breast, was there in the middle of them.

"The people must judge her," said he, and the people did. They judged that she should be put to the fire and burned.

She was taken from the high halls and put in a dark, damp cell with the wind blowing in through the barred window. Instead of silks and velvets they gave her the bundle of nettles she had gathered — she could have those for a pillow. The fierce, stinging mailed shirts of nettle that she had woven could do for quilt and coverlet but (had they known) she could have asked for nothing better. She turned back to her work and prayed to God, while outside the street-kids jeered her and not a soul spoke a word of comfort.

Towards evening there was the beating of a swan's wing against her prison bars — it was her youngest brother who'd found where his sister was. She sobbed aloud with joy even though she knew that the coming night might be the last she had to live. But her work was almost done and her brothers were here.

The archbishop came, for he had promised the king to watch over her for the last time. But she shook her head at him and urged him by her looks and gestures to leave her alone. This was the night when she would finish her work, otherwise everything would have been in vain — everything: her tears, her pain, her sleepless nights. The archbishop swore at her as he left, but poor Elise knew she was innocent and got on with her work. Little mice ran across the floor, dragging the nettles to her feet to help her, and a thrush sat by the prison bars and sang the whole night long as joyfully as he could, so as to keep her spirits up.

An hour before dawn the eleven brothers gathered at the palace gates demanding to see the king. But that could not be done. Why — it was the middle of the night, the king was still asleep, he was not to be disturbed. They begged, they threatened — the guards came and eventually even the king came himself to find out what was going on. But at that moment the sun rose — the brothers were nowhere to be seen, but eleven white swans rose up above the palace.

Everybody came flocking out of the city gates to see the burning of the witch. A spavined nag pulled the cart where she sat and they'd dressed her in a smock of coarse sacking. Her soft hair fell loose from her beautiful head, her cheeks were pale as death, her lips moved silently, but her fingers still teased the green flax. Even on the road to death she did not cease in the work she had begun; ten of the nettle-mail shirts lay at her feet, and she wove and wove at the eleventh. The crowd just mocked her.

"Look at the mumbling witch! Where's the prayerbook she ought to have? Look at the foul sorcery she's up to! Rip it out – rip it to a thousand pieces!" and they all crowded in on her to tear it apart. But out of the air flew eleven white swans. They perched round her on the cart, beat with their powerful wings, and the mob fell back in terror.

"It is a sign from heaven!" came a whisper. "She is innocent!" But no one dared to say it more loudly.

The executioner grasped her hands but at the last moment she flung the eleven shirts on to the swans and there stood eleven handsome princes. But instead of an arm, the youngest one had a swan's wing, for she hadn't been able to finish one of the sleeves of his nettle-shirt.

"Now I may speak," she said. "I am innocent."

And the crowd, when they saw what had happened, bent their knees before her as a saint, but she herself sank fainting into her brothers' arms, exhausted by so much suspense and anguish and pain. "Yes," said her eldest brother, "she is innocent," and he told how everything had happened. And as he spoke the air was filled with the scent of a million roses, for every branch in what was to have been Elise's pyre had struck down roots and put forth branches, making a great, high hedge of fragrant red roses, while above them was a blossoming white-petalled flower, gleaming like a star. This, the king plucked and set down on Elise's breast and she awoke with peace and happiness in her heart.

And all the church bells rang of their own accord, the birds flew down in great flocks and there was a wedding procession such as no king had ever had before.

THE SWINEHERD

Once upon a time there was a poor prince. He had a kingdom that was only tiny, but at least it was big enough for him to get married on and that's what he wanted – to get married.

Now you may well say that it was a bit cheeky of him to dare to say to the Emperor's daughter, "Will you have me?" But he did dare, because his name was famous far and wide and there were hundreds of princesses who would have been glad to say "yes" – but did she say that?

Well, we shall see…

On the prince's father's grave there grew a rose tree – ah, it was such a beautiful rose tree. It only bloomed once every five years and then it only bore a single rose, but what a rose that was! It smelled so sweet that whoever sniffed it forgot all his cares and troubles. What's more, he also had a nightingale that could sing as if it had all the most beautiful melodies lodged in its throat. The rose and the nightingale were both for the princess, so they were put into large silver caskets and sent off to her.

The Emperor had them carried in front of him into the great chamber where the princess went and played 'visitors' with her ladies-in-waiting – they never did anything else — and when she saw the large caskets with the presents in she clapped her hands for joy. "Perhaps it will be a little pussycat," she said — but out came the beautiful rose.

"Oh — how prettily it's made!" said all the ladies-in-waiting.

"It's more than pretty," said the Emperor, "it's really quite nice."

But the princess touched it and she was all ready to burst out crying.

"Fie, Papa!" she said. "It's not made, it's real!"

"Fie!" said all the court ladies. "It's *real!*"

"Now first of all, let's see what's in the other casket before we get cross," said the Emperor, and out came the nightingale. It sang so beautifully that, there and then, you couldn't find anything to say against it.

"*Superbe! Charmant!*" said the ladies-in-waiting, for they all spoke French — each one worse than the one before.

"How that bird reminds me of the late Empress's musical snuff box," said an old courtier. "Ah yes! it has quite the same tone, the very same expression!"

"Yes," said the Emperor, and he wept like a little child.

"Even so, I can't believe that it's real," said the princess.

"Yes, it's a real bird," said the ones who'd brought it.

"Well then, let the bird fly," said the princess, and she wouldn't let the prince come on any account.

But he wouldn't let himself be put off. He smeared his face all brown and black, pulled his hat well down on his head and knocked at the door. "Hello, Emperor," he said, "could I perhaps go into service here in the castle?"

"Ah, well, there are lots asking," said the Emperor, "but let me see — I want someone who can look after the swine; we've got a lot of them."

And so the prince was appointed Imperial Swineherd. He was given a wretched little room down by the pigsty and there he had to stay! But all day long he sat and worked, and by the evening he had made a pretty little pot with bells all round it, and when the pot boiled the bells rang out so beautifully, playing the old tune:

Oh, my darling Augustin
Everything's gone, gone, gone, gone!

But the cleverest thing about it was that if you held your finger in the steam from

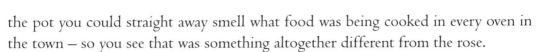

the pot you could straight away smell what food was being cooked in every oven in the town — so you see that was something altogether different from the rose.

Now the princess was out walking with all her ladies-in-waiting, and when she heard the tune she stood still and looked so pleased — for she could play 'Oh, my darling Augustin' as well — in fact it was the only tune she knew, but she played it with one finger.

"Why, that's the one I can play!" she said. "That must be a very educated swineherd. Listen! Go in and ask him how much that instrument costs."

So one of the ladies-in-waiting had to run in — but she put on her pattens. "How much do you want for the pot?" said the lady-in-waiting.

"I want ten kisses from the princess," said the swineherd.

"God preserve us!" said the lady-in-waiting.

"Yes, it can't be less," said the swineherd.

"Now — what did he say?" asked the princess.

"I really can't tell you," said the lady-in-waiting, "it's awful!"

"Then you can whisper it," and so she whispered it.

"He's very naughty!" said the princess, and went straight off — but after she'd gone a little way the bells rang out so prettily:

Oh, my darling Augustin
Everything's gone, gone, gone, gone!

"Listen!" said the princess. "Ask him if he'll have ten kisses from my ladies-in-waiting."

"No thanks!" said the swineherd. "Ten kisses from the princess or I keep the pot."

"What a tiresome business!" said the princess. "Oh, well, you'd better all stand round me so that nobody sees." And the ladies-in-waiting stood round her and spread out their dresses, and the swineherd got the ten kisses and she got the pot.

Now that was fun! Day in and day out they had the pot boiling. There wasn't an oven in the whole town where they didn't know what was cooking — neither at the chamberlain's nor at the shoemaker's. The ladies-in-waiting danced and clapped their hands, "We know who's having soup and pancakes! We know who's having chops and porridge! Oh — isn't it interesting!"

"Terribly interesting," said the mistress-of-the-queen's-bedchamber.

"Yes, but keep your mouth shut, for I'm the Emperor's daughter!"

"God preserve us," they all said.

The swineherd (that is to say the prince — but of course nobody knew that he was anything but a true swineherd) didn't let a day go by without working at something and so he made a rattle. When you whirled this round, you could hear all the waltzes, mazurkas and polkas from the very beginning of the world.

"But that is *superbe!*" said the princess as she went by. "I've never heard a more beautiful composition. Listen! Go in and ask him how much he wants for the instrument — but I'm not kissing!"

"He wants a hundred kisses from the princess," said the lady-in-waiting who'd gone in and asked him.

"I think he's mad," said the princess, and she left. But after she'd gone a little way she stopped. "One must encourage the arts," she said, "after all, I am the Emperor's daughter! Tell him he can have ten kisses like the last time, and he may take the rest from my ladies-in-waiting!"

"Oh, yes, but we'd so much rather not," said the ladies-in-waiting.

"Rubbish!" said the princess. "If I can kiss him then you can too. Just remember that I give you all board and wages." So the lady-in-waiting had to go in and see him again.

"A hundred kisses from the princess," he said, "otherwise we each keep our own."

"Stand round!!!" she said. And so all the ladies-in-waiting stood round and he began kissing.

"What's all that crowd down by the pigsties?" said the Emperor, who had stepped out on to his balcony. He rubbed his eyes and put on his spectacles. "To be sure, it's those ladies-in-waiting up to their games! I'll have to go down to them," and he pulled up the back of his slippers — for they were shoes that he'd trodden down behind.

Hey up! How he hurried!

As soon as he got into the courtyard he went very softly and the ladies-in-waiting had so much to do counting kisses (for it had to be fair and square — he mustn't have too many and he mustn't have too few) that they never noticed the Emperor. He stood on tip-toe.

"What's all this?" he said, when he saw the kissing — and he sloshed them round the head with his slipper just as the swineherd was taking his eighty-sixth kiss. "Be off!" said the Emperor, for he was angry, and both the princess and the swineherd were turned out of his empire.

So now she stood there and cried. The swineherd was scolding her and the rain

"I've never heard a more beautiful composition."

was falling down.

"Oh, what a wretched mortal I am!" said the princess. "If only I'd married that beautiful prince! Oh, how unhappy I am!"

And the swineherd went behind a tree, wiped the black and the brown from his face, threw away his dirty clothes and stepped out in all his prince's raiment, so handsome that the princess had to curtsey.

"I have come to despise you – you!" he said. "You wouldn't have an honest prince. You could not appreciate the rose and the nightingale. But you could kiss the swineherd for a musical toy. Now see what you get for it…"

And he went into his kingdom, shut the door and shot the bolt. So now she really could stand outside and sing:

Oh, my darling Augustin
Everything's gone, gone, gone, gone!

THE NIGHTINGALE

In China, you know, the Emperor's Chinese — and all the people round him, they're Chinese too. Now this happened many years ago, but that's just the reason why it's worth hearing the story — before we all forget it!

The Emperor's palace was the most magnificent in the world — utterly and entirely made of the finest porcelain — so precious, but so dainty and so delicate to touch that you had to be careful how you went. Out in the garden you could see the most wonderful flowers, and silver bells had been tied to the most beautiful ones, and these tinkled to make sure that you wouldn't go past without noticing them. Oh yes! Everything was very carefully thought out in the Emperor's garden, and it stretched so far that even the gardener didn't know where it finished. If you went on you'd come to a beautiful forest, with tall trees and deep lakes, and this forest went right down to the sea which was deep and blue. Great ships could sail right in under the branches, and here there lived a nightingale that sang so divinely that even the poor fisherman, who'd got so much else to do, stood still and listened, hearing the nightingale while he was out at night lifting his nets. "Good Lord — how she sings!" he'd say, but then he'd have so many things to do that he'd forget the bird. The next night though, when

Even the poor fisherman, who'd got so much else to do, stood still and listened

it was singing again and the fisherman came along he'd say once more, "Good Lord — just listen to that singing!"

Travellers came from all the countries of the world to the Emperor's city and they marvelled at it, and at the palace and the garden, but when they heard the nightingale they all said, "Ah, but that's the best of all!"

And the travellers told their tales about it when they got home, and the scholars wrote lots of books about the town, the palace and the garden, but they never forgot the nightingale — that always came first; and the ones with a turn for poetry would write the most beautiful poems — every one about the nightingale in the forest by the deep lake.

These books found their way round the world and it so happened that some of them once reached the Emperor. He sat in his golden chair, reading and reading, nodding his head over and over again, for he liked to hear the splendid accounts of his town, his palace and his garden. "But the nightingale, that's the best of all!" — there it was, written down.

"What's all this!" said the Emperor. "A nightingale! I've never heard of such a thing! Is there such a bird in my empire, let alone in my garden? I've never heard it. Fancy having to read about it!"

And so he summoned his chamberlain, who was so grand that if any lesser mortal dared to talk to him or ask him something he'd say nothing but "P!" for an answer — and that doesn't mean anything at all.

"Look what it says here about a most remarkable bird called a nightingale," said the Emperor, "they say that it's the best thing in the whole of my empire. Why has no one ever told me about this?"

"I have never heard it mentioned," said the chamberlain. "It has never been presented at court."

"I desire that it shall come here this evening and sing for me," said the Emperor. "The whole world seems to know what I have, and I know nothing about it!"

"I have never heard its name," said the chamberlain, "but I shall seek it and I shall find it."

But where was it to be found? The chamberlain ran up and down all the staircases, through all the rooms and passages, but nobody that he met had heard tell of the nightingale, and the chamberlain ran back to the Emperor and said that it must all be a story made up by the people who wrote books. "Your Imperial Majesty should not believe everything that is written down – it's all invention – something called the Black Art!"

"But the book where I read it," said the Emperor, "was sent to me by his Imperial Highness the Emperor of Japan, so it can't be wrong. I will hear the nightingale! It shall come here this evening! It has my most gracious favour! And if it doesn't come then the whole court shall have their stomachs trampled on after they've eaten their supper!"

"Tsing-Pe," said the chamberlain and he ran up and down all the stairs again, and through all the rooms and passages, and half the court ran with him because they didn't care to have their stomachs trampled on. There was much asking around after this amazing nightingale, who was known to the whole world, but to nobody at court.

Eventually they came upon a poor little serving-maid in the kitchen. She said, "Good Lord, the nightingale! I know all about that. My word, how it sings! Every evening they let me take a few leftovers from the table home to my poor, sick mother who's living down by the shore, and when I'm on my way back and I'm tired and I sit down to rest in the wood then I hear the nightingale singing. It brings tears to my eyes, as if my mother was kissing me."

"Little serving-maid," said the chamberlain, "I shall appoint you to a permanent place on the staff of the kitchen, and you shall be allowed to watch the Emperor eating his dinner, so long as you can lead us to the nightingale who is required for this evening."

And so everybody set out for the wood where the nightingale sang – half the court went along. They were just putting their best foot forward when a cow began to moo.

"Oh!" said an Imperial pageboy. "There it is! How amazing that such a little thing should have such powerful lungs! I've certainly heard it before."

"No – that's just a cow mooing," said the little kitchen-maid, "we're still a long way from the place."

And now some frogs croaked in the marsh.

"Delightful!" said the Chinese palace chaplain. "I can hear it now – just like little church bells!"

"No, that's just frogs," said the little kitchen-maid, "but I think we'll hear it soon."

Then the nightingale began to sing.

"There it is!" said the little kitchen-maid. "Listen! Listen! And there – just look at it!" and she pointed to a little grey bird up in the branches.

"Impossible!" said the chamberlain. "I'd never have believed such a thing! How

plain it looks! It must have lost its colour through seeing so many important people."

"Little nightingale!" called the kitchen-maid, quite loud. "Our gracious Emperor would like you to sing for him."

"With the greatest pleasure," said the nightingale, and sang so that it was wonderful to hear.

"Just like glass-bells!" said the chamberlain. "And look at its little throat, how it's going. It really is astonishing that we've never heard it before. It will have a great *succès d'estime* at court."

"Shall I sing once more for the Emperor?" said the nightingale, who thought the Emperor was there.

"My excellent little nightingale," said the chamberlain, "it gives me great pleasure to invite you to a court entertainment this evening where you shall enchant his High Imperial Majesty with your charming song."

"It sounds better in the open," said the nightingale, but it was glad to go along when it heard what the Emperor wanted.

Back at the palace there was much titivating going on! The walls and floors, which were all made of porcelain, glittered in the light of thousands of golden lamps. The most beautiful flowers, that would tinkle most clearly, were arranged in the passageways. There was so much running about, so much fluster, and the bells were all ringing so that you couldn't hear yourself speak.

In the middle of the great hall where the Emperor sat they put up a golden perch and that was for the nightingale. The whole court was assembled, and the little kitchen-maid was allowed to stand behind the door, because now she'd been given the appointment of a *real* kitchen-maid. Everyone was there in full dress and everyone watched the little grey bird as the Emperor nodded to it.

And the nightingale sang so beautifully that it brought tears to the Emperor's eyes and tears trickled down over his cheeks, and then the nightingale sang even more sweetly so that it went straight to your heart. And the Emperor was so pleased that he said the nightingale should have his golden slipper to hang round its neck. But the nightingale thanked him and said that it had already been given enough. "I have seen tears in the Emperor's eyes, that is the greatest treasure for me! An Emperor's tears have a marvellous power! God knows you have rewarded me enough," and it sang once more with its sweet, enchanting voice.

"Why, it's the most darling little lovey-dove I ever saw!" said the court-ladies all round and they filled their mouths with water so that they could gurgle when anyone spoke to them — they thought *they'd* be nightingales as well. Indeed the footmen and the chambermaids pronounced that they too were content, and that's saying a lot because they're altogether the most difficult people to satisfy. Yes, the nightingale was a complete success.

It was now to remain at court, have its own cage, with freedom to go out walking: two trips in the daytime and one at night. Twelve attendants went with it, every one of them bearing a silken ribbon attached to its leg which they hung on to good and tight. There was no fun whatsoever in an expedition like that.

The whole town was talking about the wonderful bird and whenever two people met each other, one would never say anything but "Nightin—!" and the other would say "—gale!" and then they would sigh and understand one another perfectly. Indeed, eleven tinkers' children were named after it, but not one of them had a note of music in his body.

One day a big parcel came for the Emperor, and on it was written the one word: Nightingale.

"There now, we've got a new book on our famous bird," said the Emperor — but it wasn't a book, it was a little clockwork toy packed in a box, an artificial nightingale made to look like the living one, but set all about with diamonds and rubies and sapphires. As soon as this clockwork bird was wound up it could sing one of the pieces that the real one sang and its tail would go up and down, glittering with gold and silver. Round its neck there hung a little ribbon with the message 'The Emperor of Japan's nightingale is a poor thing beside the Emperor of China's.'

"Oh, how delightful!" said everyone, and the person who'd delivered the clockwork bird was straight away appointed Chief-Imperial-Nightingale-Bringer.

"Now they must both sing together — what a duet that will be!"

And so they had to sing together, but it didn't go right at all because the real nightingale sang in its own way and the artificial bird went in waltz time. "That's not his fault," said the Master of the Emperor's Musick. "He keeps time perfectly and quite in the fashion I require." So the clockwork bird had to sing alone. He had just as much success as the real one, and what's more he was much nicer to look at, glittering away like bracelets and brooches.

Thirty-three times he sang one and the same piece, and still he wasn't tired. People would gladly have heard it all round again but the Emperor thought that the living nightingale should now sing for a little while too – but where was it? No one had noticed, but it had flown off out of the open window, back to its green forest.

"Well, but what's this!" said the Emperor, and all the court-people got cross and said that the nightingale was a most ungrateful creature. "Ah, but we have the better bird," they said, and so the clockwork bird had to sing once more, and that was the thirty-fourth time it played the same piece, but they still couldn't get it by heart because it was very difficult. And the Master of the Emperor's Musick lavished his highest praises on the bird and assured everyone that it was better than the real nightingale, not just because of its plumage and all the beautiful diamonds, but also because of its insides.

"For you see, ladies and gentlemen, and, above all, my lord Emperor, with the real nightingale you can never calculate what will come next, whereas with the artificial bird everything is fixed. It always works the same way and no other. It can be explained. You can open it up and see the engineering: how the waltzes are laid out, how they go, and how each one follows the next…"

"Just what I thought," said everyone, and the Master of the Emperor's Musick was given permission to show the bird to the people next Sunday – they might also hear it sing, said the Emperor. And they did hear it, and they were as happy as if they'd got themselves drunk on tea (for that's a very Chinese thing to do). And everyone there said, "Oh!" and lifted up a finger (the one we used to call Lick-pot) and nodded. But the poor fisherman who'd heard the real nightingale said, "It sounds nice enough, and quite a likeness too, but something's missing. I've no idea what."

The real nightingale was banished from the country and the empire.

The clockwork bird was placed on a silken cushion next to the Emperor's bed. All the presents it had been given – gold and precious stones – lay all around and it had been raised to the rank of High-Imperial-Singer-In-The-Night, Number One on the Left – for the Emperor reckoned that the most important side was the one where your heart is, and hearts are on the left even in Emperors. And the Master of the Emperor's Musick wrote a twenty-five volume account of the artificial bird. It was so long and so learned, and had all the most difficult Chinese words in it, and yet everybody said that they'd read it and understood it – otherwise they'd have been thought stupid and would have had their stomachs trampled on.

So it was that a whole year went by: the Emperor, the court and all the other

Chinamen knew every little trill in the clockwork bird's song, but for that very reason it seemed to them the best of all — they could join with it in the singing and that was just what they did. The urchins sang *"Zizizi, zizizi, cluck, cluck, cluck!"*, and even the Emperor sang... Oh, yes, it was all absolutely splendid.

But one evening, when the clockwork bird was singing its best and the Emperor was lying in bed listening to it, something inside the bird went *"svupp!"*, something else went *"whirrr!"*, all the wheels ran down and the music stopped.

The Emperor jumped straight out of bed and had his personal physician summoned — but how could *he* help? So then they sent for a watchmaker, and after a great deal of talking and a great deal of poking about he put the bird into something like order, but he said that they must now use it very carefully, for its bearings were all worn down and it wasn't possible to get new ones that would match in with the music. All this was greeted with great dismay. From now on they would only let the clockwork bird sing once a year — and even that was almost too much. But the Master of the Emperor's Musick gave a lecture full of difficult words saying that everything *was* just as good as before, so everything *was* just as good as before.

By now five years had gone by and the whole country was plunged in grief — for, on the whole, everyone was fond of the Emperor, but now he was sick and (so it was said) not likely to live. A new Emperor had already been chosen and people stood outside in the streets and asked the chamberlain how things went with the old one.

"P!" he said, and shook his head.

The Emperor lay cold and pale in his great, magnificent bed. The whole court thought that he was dead, and each of them ran off to greet the new Emperor. The chambermaids ran out to gossip about it, and the palace serving-maids had a great coffee party. In all the rooms and passages heavy cloth had been unrolled so that no one could be heard walking, and this meant that it was all so quiet... so quiet...

But the Emperor was not dead yet. He lay there, stiff and pale, in his magnificent bed with its long velvet curtains and its heavy gold tassels; and high up there was a window standing open, with the moon shining in on the Emperor and the clockwork bird.

The poor Emperor could scarcely breathe — it was as if he had something on his chest. He opened his eyes and saw that it was Death who sat there on his chest. He had put on the Emperor's golden crown and he held in one hand his golden sword and in the other his splendid banner; and all round in the folds of the great velvet curtains of the bed there stared out strange faces, some ugly and others wonderfully kind. These were all the Emperor's good and bad deeds who looked down on him now that Death sat over his heart.

"Do you remember this?" they whispered one after the other. "Do you remember this!" and they told him so much that the sweat stood out on his forehead.

"But I never knew that!" said the Emperor. Then, "Music! Music! The big Chinese drum!" he shouted. "So that I shall not hear these things they are saying!"

And they went on, and Death nodded like a Chinaman at all that they said.

"Music! Music!" shrieked the Emperor. "You wonderful little golden bird, sing now! Sing! I have given you gold and precious things. I have myself hung my golden slipper round your neck. Now sing! Sing!"

But the bird stood silent. There was no one to wind him up and he couldn't sing without that. But Death went on looking at the Emperor out of the large, hollow sockets of his eyes and it was so quiet... so terribly quiet...

Then, at that moment, there sounded close by the window the most beautiful song. It was the little, living nightingale, sitting on the branches outside. It had heard about the Emperor's need and had come to sing to him of comfort and hope. And as he sang the phantoms grew paler and paler, the blood ran faster and faster in the Emperor's weak body, and Death himself listened and said, "Go on, little nightingale, go on!"

"Ah, yes – will you give me the splendid golden sword! Ah, yes – will you give me the rich banner! Will you give me the Emperor's crown!"

And Death gave up these treasures for a song, and the nightingale sang on and on. It sang of the quiet churchyard, where the white roses grow, where the elder-blossom scents the air, and where the fresh grass is watered by the tears of the mourners. Then Death began to long for his garden and he floated out of the window like a cold, white mist.

"Thank you, oh thank you! You heavenly little bird," said the Emperor. "I know you now. I hunted you out of my country and my empire, and yet you have sung the evil spirits from my bed and driven Death from my heart. How can I reward you?"

"You *have* rewarded me," said the nightingale, "I brought tears to your eyes the first time I sang; I shall never forget that of you! Those are the jewels that lift a singer's heart. But sleep now and get well and strong again! I shall sing for you."

And it sang — and the Emperor fell into a sweet sleep, a kindly, refreshing sleep.

When he awoke, strengthened and in health again, the sun was shining down through the windows. None of his servants had come back again yet, for they all thought that he was dead, but the nightingale still stayed there and sang.

"You must stay with me always," said the Emperor. "You shall sing what you like and as for this clockwork bird, I shall break it in a thousand pieces."

"Don't do that," said the nightingale, "he has done the best he could. Keep him by you as before. I can't build my nest and live in the palace, but let me come whenever I've a mind to come and then, in the evening, I'll sit in the branches outside the window and sing for you so that you may be at once contented and full of wise thoughts. I shall sing about those who are happy and those who suffer; I shall sing about the evil and the good that are hidden around you. Little singing-birds fly far afield — to the poor fisherman, to the peasant's roof, to everyone who lives far from you and your court. I love your heart more than your crown — and yet your crown has the air of something holy about it. I'll come, I'll sing for you! But you must promise me this..."

"Anything," said the Emperor, and stood there in his Imperial robes, that he had put on himself, and he held his sword, heavy with gold, to his heart.

"One thing I beg of you. Don't mention to anyone that you have a little bird that tells you everything — that way everything will be better."

And the nightingale flew away.

The servants came in to attend to their dead Emperor — yes, there they stood, and the Emperor said, "Good morning!"

The Ugly Duckling

Ah, yes, it was very delightful out in the countryside. It was summertime. The corn was yellow, the oats green, the hay stacked up in the green meadows, and over there strutted the stork on his long red legs, chattering away in Egyptian, which he'd got from his mother. All around the fields and meadows were the great woodlands and, in the middle of the woodlands, deep lakes. Ah, yes, it really was very delightful out there in the country.

Lying out there in the sunshine was an old manor house with deep homemade ponds all around it, and from its walls down to the water were huge dock leaves, so tall that little children could stand upright under the biggest ones. Ooh, it was a bit of a jungle in there – you'd think you were deep in the woods – but it was just there that a duck had made a nest to hatch out her ducklings. She was getting very bored with it though; it was all taking a long time, and she didn't get many visitors. The other ducks would rather swim around in the ponds than waddle up under a lot of dock leaves just for a gossip.

Finally one egg after another cracked open. *"Chip, chip!"* they'd cry, and in every eggshell was a little creature sticking out its head.

"*Rap, rap!*" she said, and they all quackled as best they could and looked around under the green leaves and their mama let them look around as much as they liked, for green is very good for the eyes.

"Wow, the world's a big place," said all the young'uns, since they had a deal more room here than they'd had in their eggshells.

"And do you think that's the whole world?" asked Mama. "Why, it goes from here right to the other side of the garden to the parson's field, although, myself, I was never over that way. Now, are we all present and correct?" and she got up to go. "Oh, no we are not!" she said. "That big one's still there. How much longer have we got to hang about? I'm fed up with waiting." And she sat down again.

"Well, what's going on?" said an old duck, who'd come to pay a visit.

"We're hanging about for this last egg," said the duck, still sitting down. "It won't get itself broken — but come on, have a look at these others. Aren't they just the duckiest little ducks you ever did see? They're the image of their daddy, the old so-and-so, never coming to see me!"

"Let me have a look at that egg, the one that won't break," said the old duck. "I wouldn't mind betting it's a turkey egg. I had a lot of trouble and grief over those one time, for the young'uns were frightened of the water. I'm telling you — I couldn't get 'em to go in! I quacked and snapped at 'em but that wasn't no use at all. Let me look at that egg. Yeah — that's a turkey egg. Just leave it there and teach the other kids to swim!"

"Well, I'll sit on it for a while, since I've sat for so long," said the duck. "See you at Christmas!"

"If that's what you want," said the old duck and went off.

Eventually the big egg broke. "*Chip, chip!*" said the little'un, and climbed out. He was very large and ugly. The duck looked at him. "That's a horrid big duckling," she said, "he don't look a bit like the others. Perhaps he is a turkey-chick? Well — we'll soon find out. He's going in the water if I have to kick him in myself!"

Next day, the weather was blessedly warm with the sun shining down through the green dock leaves. The mother duck brought her family down to the pond and "*splash!*" she jumped into the water. "*Quack, quack!*" she said, and one duckling after another plumped in after her. The water went right over their heads but they popped up again quick and swam off charmingly — all in the water with their legs going like clockwork.

Even the little ugly grey one swam along too.

"Well," she said, "that's no turkey. Just look how prettily his legs go and how well he carries himself. He's one of mine all right and he's really quite handsome if you look at him from the right angle. *Quack, quack* – come along with me, all of you, into the big world, and I'll introduce you to everyone in the duck-yard. But stay close in case anyone treads on you, and watch out for the cat!"

And so they arrived at the duck-yard where there was a great racket going on with two families fighting over an eel-head, which the cat got after all.

"There!" said Mama. "You can see what goes on in the world," and she licked her beak since she'd have liked the eel-head too. "Get your legs going, quack around a bit and see that you make a bow to that old duck over there. She tops everyone here. She has Castilian blood in her, which is why she's so fat, and if you look you can see that she's got a red rag on her leg. That is extraordinarily grand, the most remarkable distinction for any duck in the yard. It means she's not to be lost and is to be picked out above everyone, man or beast. Quack away now – don't turn your toes in! A well-brought-up duckling turns its toes out from the back just like its pa and ma! Look! Now bow your heads and say 'Quack!'"

And that's what they did, but the other ducks standing around took one look at them and said quite loud, "Ooer – look at that! Now we've got that lot here, as though there weren't enough of us already! And, good grief! Look at that one over there! He's a sight! We won't put up with him" – and one duck flew at him and bit him in the neck.

"Just you let him be," said his ma. "He's not done anything to you!"

"Yeah, but he's too big and funny-looking," said the duck who'd bitten him, "so he needs shoving around."

"That mother's got some nice little things," said the old duck with the rag round her leg, "all pretty except that one there who's not a success. I'd hope she could do something about him."

"That can't be done, Your Grace," said the mother-duck, "he's not beautiful, but he's good-tempered and he swims well – yes, I'd say better than the others. Yes, I think he'll grow up nicely and get a bit smaller in time. He was too long in his egg so he hasn't got quite the right shape," and she pinched his neck and smoothed his feathers. "You can see he's a drake," she said, "so it won't matter too much. I reckon he's strong enough; he'll do all right."

"The other ducklings are very pretty," said the old duck, "so make yourselves at home — and if you find an eel-head, bring it along to me."

And so they made themselves at home.

But the poor duckling, who'd been last out of his egg and looked so ugly, was bitten and shoved around and made a fool of just as much by the ducks as by the hens. "He's just too big," they all said, and the turkey-cock, who'd been born with spurs on and thus strutted around as though he were the Kaiser, puffed himself up like a ship in full sail, shouldered his way up to him, gobbled at him, and went red in the face. The poor duckling scarcely knew whether to stand or to walk and was wretchedly upset over being so ugly and being scoffed at by everyone in the duck-yard.

That was merely what happened on the first day and after that things just got worse and worse. The poor thing was chased around by them all, and even his brothers and sisters turned on him, saying, "Let's hope the cat gets you, you horrible fright!", and his mother said, "I wish you'd clear off!", and the ducks bit him, the hens pecked him, and even the girl who came to feed the poultry gave him a kicking.

So he ran off and flew over the fence, frightening the little birds in the hedge who flew up into the air. "Well, I suppose that's because I'm so ugly," thought the duckling, and he shut his eyes but carried on going. That took him to a big fen where the wild ducks lived and there he spent the night full of sorrow and grief.

Next morning the wild ducks came along to see this new chum. "Who do you think you are then?" they asked. The duckling showed himself off and bowed to them as best he could.

"You're remarkably ugly," said the wild ducks, "but that makes no odds to us so long as you don't try to marry any of us." Oh, the poor old thing! He wasn't after marrying anyone — he just wanted to be allowed to sit in the reeds and drink a bit of the marsh-water.

He lay there for a full two days and then a couple of wild geese turned up — or, at least, wild ganders, for they were a couple of chaps. They'd not long been out of their eggs themselves, which may account for them being a bit cheeky.

"Look here, pal," said one of them, "you're so ugly that I've really taken a fancy to you! Why don't you come with us and do travelling? Over there, in a bit of the marsh just across the way there are some very pretty wild geese — not one of them spoken for — you could take your pick even if you are ugly."

PIFF! PAFF! cracked out at that very moment and the two wild geese fell dead among the reeds and the water turned blood-red. PIFF! PAFF! – again – and a great flock of wild geese flew up out of the reeds and it all went on and on. There was a big shoot happening. The hunters had surrounded the marsh – some even getting up into the branches of the trees that stretched out over the reeds. Clouds of blue smoke drifted among the dark branches and hung over the water. Hunting dogs – *rrraff, rrraff!* – came through, heaving the reeds and rushes to one side. This was terrifying for the poor duckling who tried to put his head under his wing, but at that moment a frightful big dog arrived with its tongue hanging out half way down its chest and its eyes gleaming gruesomely. It nosed itself at the duckling, bared its sharp teeth and then – *splash! splash!* – passed on by without grabbing him.

"God be thanked!" sighed the duckling to himself. "I'm so ugly that even the dogs can't stand to sink their teeth into me," and he lay there very quietly while shots rang out through the reeds and gun after gun after gun went off.

Much later in the day things quietened down but the poor little young'un didn't dare to get up and he waited there some hours before looking all round and then making off out of the fen as fast as he could. He ran across fields and meadows but a storm had blown up and he had a job making much headway.

Come evening he found himself at a broken-down old hut. This was so dilapidated that it couldn't make up its mind which way to fall over, so it was still standing up. The storm whirled round the little duckling so strongly that he had to sit on his tail feathers to keep himself upright and it just blew worse and worse. Then suddenly he noticed that one of the hinges of the door was broken and it was hanging so crookedly that he could creep into the room, and that he did.

An old woman lived there with a cat and a hen. The cat, who was called Sonny Boy, could arch his back and purr. What's more he could give out sparks, but for that you had to stroke him the wrong way. The hen had little short legs and was known as Skinnimalinki-shortshanks. She was very good at laying eggs and the old woman loved her as her own child.

In the morning they all saw the visiting duckling straight away and the cat began to purr and the hen to cluck.

"What's all this then?" said the old woman, peering about, for she didn't see too well and thought that the little duckling was a full-size duck that had got lost. "That's

Come evening he found himself at a broken-down old hut

a great catch," she said, "now I can get a duck egg, unless it's a drake – we'll have to have a look-see."

So the duckling was given a three-week trial – but there weren't any eggs. And the cat was master of the house and the hen mistress, and they always liked to say of themselves "We and the World", for they thought that they were a half of it, and the best half too. The duckling thought you could have a different opinion, but the hen would have none of it.

"Can you lay eggs?" she asked.

"No."

"Well then, hold your tongue."

And the cat said, "Can you arch your back and give out sparks?"

"No."

"Then don't come here with your opinions when sensible people are speaking."

So the duckling sat in a corner in a black mood, but then he began to think of the fresh air and the sunshine and he conceived a desperate desire to get to some water, and he couldn't help telling the hen about it.

"What on earth's got into you?" asked the hen. "You've got nothing to do – that's why you get these ideas. Lay an egg or purr, then you'll get over it."

"But it would be wonderful to float in the water," said the duckling, "wonderful to let it come over your head and dabble down to the bottom."

"Oh, yes," said the hen, "that would be *really* wonderful, I must say. You've gone barmy. Just ask the cat – he's the cleverest person I know – ask him if he wants to go jumping in the water and dipping his head in it! I'll not speak for myself. Just ask the boss, our old lady – there's no one cleverer than her in the whole world – d'you think she wants to go head over heels into the water?"

"You don't understand me," said the duckling.

"Not understand you? Who's here to understand you? You can't say that there's anyone cleverer than the cat or the woman (as I said, I'll not speak for myself). Don't put on airs, child, but thank your maker for all the kindness you've received. Haven't you come here into a nice warm room, mixing with people who can teach you something? But you're a twaddler and it's by no means a pleasure to have you here. Trust me – I'm saying all this for your own good. You may think I'm being disagreeable but that's how you find who your true friends are. Now come on – lay an egg or learn to purr and give off sparks!"

"I think I'll go out into the wide world," said the duckling.

"All right – you just do that. Clear off!" said the hen.

So the duckling left. He paddled on the water, he dipped his head, but of all animals he was the odd one out because of his ugliness.

And now the autumn came. Leaves in the woodlands turned yellow and brown, the wind caught them so that they danced around, and there was a coldness in the upper air. Clouds hung heavy with the promise of hail and snowflakes, and ravens stood on the fence crying *"Snark! Snark!"*, for it was very cold. To be sure, you could almost freeze for thinking about it and the poor little duckling took no joy from it at all.

One evening, as the sun was setting in all its glory, a flock of large, beautiful birds came out of the undergrowth. The duckling had never seen anything so gorgeous: dazzling white all over, with long curving necks – they were swans, and they uttered a strange cry, spread their splendid wings, and flew away from that chilly region, off to warmer lands with unfrozen lakes. They climbed high, oh, so high, and the ugly little duckling was strangely moved as he watched them. He turned round and round in the water, like a wheel, raised his neck towards their flight, and uttered a cry so loud and strange that he frightened himself with it. Oh, he could not forget those wonderful birds and when he could no longer see them, he plunged down to the bottom of the lake and when he came up again he was simply out of himself. He did not know what these birds were nor where they were flying, but he felt for them as he had never felt for any other. There was no envy in this – how could he think of desiring such beauty for himself – why, he'd have been glad enough if the other ducks would put up with him, the poor, ugly creature.

And the winter got cold – oh, so cold. The duckling had to swim around in the water to stop it from freezing, but every night his patch of water got smaller and smaller. It froze so that the ice crackled all round and the duckling had to keep his legs moving in the water. Eventually, though, he was exhausted. He could do no more and was frozen into the ice.

Early next morning, a labourer came along. He saw what had happened and smashed the ice to pieces with one of his clogs, and took the bird back to his wife. That brought the duckling round.

The children wanted to play with him but the duckling thought they were going to hurt him and flew up in a fright, knocking the milk-pan so that the milk splashed out into the room. The woman squawked, throwing her hands up in the air so he flew down to the butter-tub and then down into the meal-tub and out again. What a sight it was! The woman shrieked and tried to hit him with the fire-irons and the children tumbled over each other after the duckling, laughing and screaming. It was a good job that the door was open and he ran out into the bushes and the new-fallen snow. There he collapsed in exhaustion.

Oh, but it would be altogether too distressing to recount all the hardships and misery he had to suffer through that hard winter. He lay in the marsh among the reeds till the sun began to get more warmth to it. Then larks sang and it was spring.

Suddenly he raised his wings to fly. They beat the air more strongly than ever before and carried him away with great power, so that before he realised what was happening he found himself in a great garden where apple trees were in full blossom and the fragrant lilacs hung their long green branches over the curving pools. Oh, wow! How very delicious it was here in all the freshness of the springtime! And there in front of him three beautiful white swans emerged from a thicket, floating, with rustling plumage, so gracefully on the water. The duckling recognised their majesty and was moved by a strange melancholy.

"I will fly over to them, those royal birds, and they'll probably strike me down – ugly me – for daring to come near them. But so what? Better to be killed by them than harried by the ducks, pecked by the hens, kicked by the girl that goes through the duck-yard and then freeze to death in the winter." Then he flew over to the pool and swam up to those splendid swans and they in turn glided toward him with rustling feathers. "Kill me quickly," said the poor creature, bowing his head towards the surface of the pool and awaiting the death-stroke – but what did he see there in the clear water? Below him he saw his own image: no longer an ungainly, greyish bird – nasty and ugly – but himself a swan.

For it makes no odds being born in a duck-yard if you come out of a swan's egg!

He felt extraordinarily glad at the hardships and the misfortunes that he had suffered; they sharpened his joy at the happiness and delight that greeted him. And the great swans swam round him, stroking him with their beaks.

Some little children came into the garden, throwing corn and breadcrumbs into the water, and the youngest called out, "Hey – there's a new one," and the others joined him, "Yes – there's a new one come!" and they clapped their hands and danced around and ran after their father and mother, still chucking bread and cake into the water. And everybody said, "That new one's the best — he's so young and pretty!" and the old swans bowed to him.

Then he felt himself very bashful and stuck his head under his wing, not knowing what to do with himself. Happy as he was, he wasn't proud (good-hearted people just don't get proud). He thought how he'd been bullied and despised and now he heard everyone say that he was the handsomest of all handsome birds. And the lilacs bent their branches toward him in the water, the sun was so warm and so comforting. He rattled his feathers, lifted his slender neck, and rejoiced in his heart, "I never dreamed of such happiness when I was an ugly duckling!"

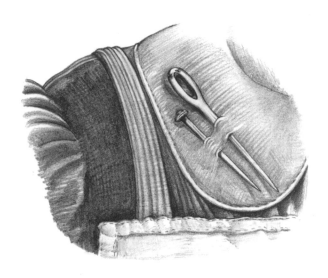

THE DARNING NEEDLE

Once upon a time there was a darning needle who was so altogether fine that she fancied she was a sewing needle.

"Watch out how you hold me," said the darning needle to the fingers that had picked her up. "Don't drop me. I'm that fine that if ever I fall on the floor I'll never be found again."

"That's as may be," said the fingers, and they pinched her round her middle.

"Watch out! Here I come with my train!" said the darning needle, and she drew a long thread after her – but it didn't have a knot at the end.

The fingers steered the needle towards the cook's slipper, where the upper leather had split and needed sewing together again.

"This is menial work," said the darning needle. "I'll not go again – I'm breaking!" – and so she broke. "Didn't I say so?" said the darning needle. "I am too fine."

Now she's good for nothing, thought the fingers, but they still had to hold her tight while the cook dipped sealing wax on to her and stuck her into the front of her neckerchief.

"Just look – now I'm a brooch," said the darning needle. "I always knew I was bound for higher things — if one is something then one will *become* something!" and she laughed to herself inside (for you can't see a darning needle laughing from the outside); and there she sat, looking round on all sides, as proud as if she were driving along in a carriage.

"May I have the honour to inquire if you are gold?" she asked the pin, who was next to her. "You look very pretty and you've got a head of your own, even if it is a little one. You must see if you can grow a bit, although it's not everyone who gets sealing-wax dropped on their end." And the darning needle drew herself up so proudly that she fell out of the apron and into the sink just as the cook was rinsing it out.

"Now we're going on our travels," said the darning needle, "I hope I don't get lost" — but she did.

"I am too fine for this world," she said as she lay in the gutter, "but I have my good conscience and that's always a small comfort." And the darning needle held herself erect and never lost her composure.

All kinds of things sailed over her: sticks, straw, bits of old newspaper. "See how they sail along!" said the darning-needle. "None of them knows what's sticking up under them. I'm the one that's sticking up! I'm the one that's sitting here! Look now — there goes a stick, and it hasn't got a thought in the world except 'stick' — and that's just itself. There goes a straw: see how it swirls, see how it twirls! Don't you think about yourself so much or you'll run into the kerb! There goes a paper — everything's forgotten that's been printed on it and yet it still thinks well of itself! Ah well, I sit here patiently and quietly. I know what I am and I'm staying that way!"

One day something came along beside her that shone so prettily the darning needle thought it was a diamond — but it was a bit of broken bottle; and because it was shining the darning needle talked to it (giving herself out to be a brooch): "I suppose you're a diamond then?"

"Oh yes, something like that!" And so each one thought the other to be a person of quality, and they talked together about how conceited the world was.

"Oh yes, I've lived in a lady's box," said the darning needle, "and the lady was a cook. She had five fingers on each hand, but I have never known anything so stuck-up as those five fingers, and yet they were only there to hold me — pick me out of the box, lay me back in the box!"

"Did they have brilliant connections?" asked the bit of bottle.

"Brilliant connections?!" said the darning needle. "Good heavens, no! But they were very conceited. They were five brothers, all born 'Finger', and they all stuck by each other even though they were different sizes: the one at the end, Thumbkin, was short and fat. He was the one who went on the outside, so he had only one joint in his back and could only make a single bow, but he used to say that if he was chopped off a man then that meant the whole of the man was no good for fighting in wars. Lickpot used to find his way into sweet things and bitter things; he could point to the sun and the moon, and he was the one who did the work when they went in for writing. Long-man looked out over the heads of the others. Goldie went around with a gold ring round his tummy, and Little Peter Play-boy didn't do anything at all, and was proud of the fact. They'd brag about this and brag about that, so I cleared off down the sink."

"And now we sit here winking," said the bit of glass — and at that moment a lot more water gushed down the gutter so that it overflowed its banks and the bit of glass was carried away.

"There! Now he's gone off to higher things!" said the darning needle. "But I stay sitting here. I really am too fine, but I'm proud to be so and that's a matter for respect." And so she sat there stiffly and thought many thoughts.

"I could almost believe that I was born of a sunbeam, I am so fine. Doesn't it seem that the sunbeams are always seeking me out under the water? Ah! I'm so fine that even my mother wouldn't be able to find me! If I had my old eye, that broke off, I think I might even weep — No! Heaven forbid that I should — weeping is just not refined!"

One day a couple of street urchins lay grubbing about in the gutter where they used to find old nails, pennies and suchlike things. It was pretty mucky but they enjoyed it very much.

"Ow!" said one of them — he'd pricked himself on the darning needle. "What sort of a feller's that?"

"I'm not a 'feller' — I'm a lady," said the darning needle, but nobody heard her. Her sealing wax was all gone and she'd turned black — but black makes you look slim and so she thought she was even finer than before.

"Here — there's an eggshell sailing down there!" said the boys, and so they stuck the darning needle into the shell.

"White walls – and I'm black," said the darning needle, "how very fetching! Now they can see me – but let's hope I don't get seasick, then I should break!" But she didn't get seasick so she didn't break.

"A steel stomach's a good thing for seasickness, and so is the knowledge that one is rather more than an ordinary person! I *do* feel better! Ah, yes – the finer one is the more one can bear."

"Crack!" said the eggshell as a wagon went over it. "Hoo! What a squeeze!" said the darning needle. "Now I shall be seasick! I'm breaking! I'm breaking!" But she didn't break even though the wagon went over her. She lay there at full length – and there she can stay!

THE RED SHOES

There was once a little girl – very slender and comely – but she was so poor that in summertime she had to go barefoot, and in winter had only clumping wooden clogs that made her ankles red and sore, which was altogether hateful.

Now, down in the village there lived an old cobbler's missus, sitting and sewing as best she could at a strip of old red cloth, making a little pair of shoes. They were clumsy things, but kindly meant, for they were being done for Karen, our little girl. These red shoes were finished and had their first outing on the very day when the little girl's mother was to be buried. That was hardly proper, but she didn't have anything else, so she put them on to follow the pauper's coffin with her mother lying in it.

Just then a big old carriage came along with a big old lady sitting in it. She saw the little girl and, taking pity on her, said to the priest, "Look here, let me take the little girl and I'll look after her."

Karen thought that this was all down to the red shoes, but the old lady said they were frightful and had them put in the fire. As for Karen herself, she was dressed up very smart. She learned to read and to sew, and people said she was very pretty. But her mirror told her, "You are much more than pretty; you are beautiful."

Round about that time the queen was travelling round the country and had her little daughter with her, who was a princess. People flocked to the castle where they were staying, with Karen among them, and the princess stood at the window in a splendid white dress so that everyone could see her. She wasn't wearing a train or a gold crown, but she had on a pair of slippers of red morroco leather, somewhat posher for sure than what the cobbler's missus had made for Karen. Oh, there's nothing in the world like red shoes!

By now, Karen had reached an age when she could be confirmed. She was to have new clothes and some new shoes as well. The best shoemaker in the town took the measure of her little foot, up in a room in his very own house, and there she saw a big glass cabinet full of pretty shoes and glossy boots. It all looked very tempting, but the old lady didn't see too well so didn't take much pleasure in it. Bang in the middle of the cabinet there was a pair of red shoes just like the ones the princess had on. Ooof — they were something! And the shoemaker said they'd been made for the daughter of a Count but hadn't fitted properly.

"That's a very glossy leather," said the old lady, "they're all shiny."

"Yes, they are shiny," said Karen, and since they fitted her, they were bought. But the old lady could not see that they were red, for she certainly wouldn't have let Karen go to her confirmation in red shoes. But that's just what Karen did.

Everybody looked at her feet, and when she went up the nave to the entrance to the choir it seemed to her that the pictures over the tombs — the portraits of the priests and the wives of the priests in their stiff collars and their long black garments — fixed their eyes on her red shoes, and that's all she thought of too. When the priest laid his hand on her head and spoke the sacred words that dedicated her to God as a true Christian, and when the organ played so solemnly, and when the voices of the pretty choirboys carolled out, and when the old cantor sang — why, all that Karen could think about was her red shoes.

That afternoon, the old lady heard from everyone about those shoes being red and she said how naughty and improper Karen was and that in future she must go to church in black shoes, however old they might be.

Well next Sunday was Holy Communion and Karen looked at the black shoes and she looked at the red. Then she looked at the red ones again and put them on.

It was a beautiful sunny day and Karen and the old lady walked to church across the fields – a rather dusty journey. By the church door there was an old soldier leaning on a crutch. He had a long beard which was more red than white – well, it was pretty well all red – and I suppose he must have been an old soldier, but he looked odd: a big, gaunt, ungainly man but with fine fingers. He bent himself almost down to the ground and asked the old lady if he might dust off her shoes. So Karen stretched out her little foot too. "Ah, what pretty little dancing shoes!" said the man who might have been a soldier. "Stay fast when you dance." And he tapped the soles with his hand. And the old lady gave the soldier a penny-piece and she and Karen went into the church.

Everyone there saw Karen's red shoes. All the portraits saw them, and when Karen kneeled at the altar and set the golden chalice to her lips she thought only of her red shoes, and it seemed to her that they were reflected in the chalice. And she forgot to sing the hymn, and she forgot to say the 'Our Father'.

Now everyone came out of church and the old lady got into her carriage. Karen was lifting her foot to follow her when the old soldier, who was standing by, said: "Oh what pretty little dancing shoes!" and Karen couldn't help it but she had to make a dance-step. Then her feet began to dance as though the shoes were making them do it and she danced off round the corner of the church – she just couldn't help it. The coachman had to run after her, pick her up and dump her in the carriage, but her feet kept dancing so that she kicked out hard at the dear old lady. In the end they got the shoes off and her legs stopped kicking.

Back home they put the shoes in a cupboard but Karen couldn't help going to look at them.

Then the old lady fell ill and they said there was no curing her. She had to be cared for and nursed and that was no one's job more than it was Karen's. But – oh! – down in the town a great ball was announced and Karen was invited. She looked at the old lady who was beyond curing, she looked at the red shoes, and it seemed to her that there was no harm in it. She took down the red shoes and put them on, went down to the ball and began to dance.

But when she danced to the right the shoes danced to the left, and when she wanted to go up the dance-floor the shoes wanted to go down – down the stairs, down through the streets and out through the city gate. Dance she did and dance she must, right out into the dark forest. Something was shining up in the trees and she thought

Dance she did and dance she must

it was the moon because it seemed to have a face, but it was the old soldier with the red beard. He sat up there and nodded to her and said, "See those pretty little dancing shoes."

Then she was really frightened and tried to kick off the red shoes, but they were stuck and although she tore off her stockings the shoes had grown fast to her feet. Dance she did and dance she must, over fields and meadows, through sun and rain, by day and by night, and the nights were the most terrifying of all.

She danced into the open churchyard, but the dead did not dance, having better things to do; she wanted to sit down by the paupers' graves, where the bitter tansy grows, but there was no rest or comfort for her. And when she danced through the open church door she saw an angel standing there in a long white gown with wings that stretched from his shoulders down to the ground. His face was stern and grave, and he held a shining broadsword in his hand.

"Thou shalt dance!" he said. "Dance in thy red shoes till thou art faint and cold, till thy skin shrivels thee into a bundle of bones! Thou shalt dance from door to door, and wheresoever there are proud and vain children thou shalt beat on the door that they may hear you and fear you. Thou shalt dance... dance... dance...!"

"Mercy!" cried Karen, but she heard no answer from the angel for her shoes carried her once more out through the gate, out over the fields, along roads and tracks, dancing as she had to.

And one morning she danced past a door she knew well. The sound of a hymn rose from inside and a coffin was brought out, all painted with flowers, and she saw that the old lady was dead. "Now," she thought, "I am abandoned by all and condemned by the Angel of the Lord."

Dance she did, and dance she must, dancing through the pitch-black night. The shoes carried her over thorns and briars, scratching till she bled. She danced over a wide heath to a little lonesome house where she knew the executioner lived and she tapped with her fingers on the window panes.

"Come out!... Come out!... I can't come in for I must dance!" And the executioner said, "Why — don't you know who I am? I chop the heads off wicked people and you can hear my axe ringing with the blows."

"Well, don't chop my head off," said Karen, "for then I shall never repent of my sins, but chop off my feet and these red shoes!"

And she confessed all her sins, and the executioner chopped off her feet with the red shoes on, and the little feet in their red shoes danced over the fields and into the dark forest. Then he fashioned some wooden feet for her with a pair of crutches, taught her the hymn that the condemned men always sing, and she kissed the hand that had wielded the axe and set off back over the heath.

"Now I've suffered enough for those red shoes," she said to herself, "so I'll go to church and people can see me," and she made for the church door. But as she got near the red shoes came dancing in front of her and she turned back in terror.

All the next week she was full of sorrow and wept many bitter tears, but with Sunday she again said to herself, "Very well, I've suffered and struggled enough. I reckon I'm just as good as plenty of people who sit in that church, putting on airs," and she set off in good heart. But once again, she wasn't far from the church gate when she saw the red shoes dancing in front of her and she turned back terrified and with remorse in her heart.

She went to the parsonage and asked if she might be taken into service there. She'd work hard and do all she could and, as for wages, all she wanted was a roof over her head and the company of good people. Well, the priest's wife pitied her and gave her a job, and she was indeed industrious and thoughtful, sitting silent in the evenings when the priest read aloud from the Bible. All the little ones were fond of her, but when they talked about fancy clothes and finery and queening it around she would shake her head.

The next Sunday they were all going to church and they asked her if she would like to go with them, but she pointed sadly to her crutches with tears in her eyes. So they all left to hear God's word while she went alone to her little room. It was only big enough to have a bed and a chair in it and she sat there with her hymn book and, as she read it in a spirit of holiness, the sound of the organ was borne over to her from the church. She raised her face, with tears in her eyes, saying, "Oh God, please help me."

The sun shone with a great brightness and there before her stood the Angel of God in his white gown, he whom she'd seen at the church door that night. But he no longer held his sharp sword but rather a green branch full of roses, and he touched the ceiling with it and that opened itself out to the heavens with a golden star shining where he touched it. And he touched the walls and they too opened out and she saw the organ playing, saw those old pictures of the priests and the wives of the priests, saw the congregation sitting in their decorated pews singing from their hymn books.

For the church had brought itself here to the poor girl in her little narrow room. Or else she had brought herself to the church. She sat in the pew among the other worshippers and when they had finished with their singing and looked up they nodded toward her and said, "It was right that you came, Karen!"

"It was grace," said she.

And the organ boomed, and the children's voices in the choir were pure and beautiful. Radiant sunshine poured its warmth through the windows and into the pew where Karen was sitting. Her heart was so full of sunshine, and peace, and joy that it broke within her. Her soul flew through the sun's glory up to God — and nobody at all asked about the Red Shoes.

THE LITTLE MATCH GIRL

Oooh! It was bitter cold. It was snowing and the evening was beginning to draw in – the last one of the year: New Year's Eve.

A raggedy little girl was going through the cold, dark streets, bare-headed and with nothing on her feet. For sure she'd had slippers on when she left home but they hadn't been much use. They were great big slippers that belonged to her mother – that's how big they were – and she'd lost them when she was crossing the street as two carriages came hurtling by. She couldn't find one of them and the other had been pinched by a little boy. He said it'd make a nice cradle if he ever had any children of his own.

So now the little girl went along with her small feet quite bare, and all red and blue with cold. She carried matches in the pocket of an old apron and had a bundle in her hand, but no one had bought anything from her the whole day. No one had given her a brass farthing. Famished and frozen, the poor little thing went along in utter misery. Snowflakes fell into her long, fair hair which curled down prettily over her neck, but this was no time for thinking about that. Lights were shining in all the windows, the streets were filled with the smell of roasted goose, for this was New Year's Eve. That *was* something to think about.

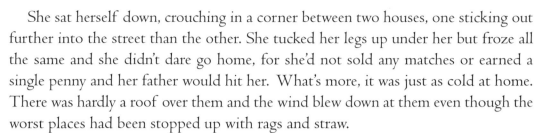

She sat herself down, crouching in a corner between two houses, one sticking out further into the street than the other. She tucked her legs up under her but froze all the same and she didn't dare go home, for she'd not sold any matches or earned a single penny and her father would hit her. What's more, it was just as cold at home. There was hardly a roof over them and the wind blew down at them even though the worst places had been stopped up with rags and straw.

Her little hands were almost dead with cold, but — hey! A match might help a little. Did she dare to pull one out of her bundle, strike it on the wall and warm her fingers?

She pulled one out. *R-r-r-itsch* — how it sputtered — how it burnt. It gave a warm, clear flame, like a little candle that she could hold her hands round — a wonderful little light. It seemed to the little girl that she sat in front of a great iron stove with bright brass feet and a bright brass cover. What a blessing the warmth was, and she stretched out both her feet to warm them too... but then the flame guttered, the oven vanished, and she was left with the little stump of the burnt-out match in her hand.

So she struck another. As it flamed up its light fell on the wall and she saw into a room, as through a veil. There was a table spread with a pure white cloth, laid out with the best china, and in the middle was a roast goose, stuffed with prunes and apples. But what was truly wondrous was that the goose hopped off the table and waddled towards the little girl with the carving-knife and fork in its back. Then the match went out and all she could see was the thick, cold wall.

So she struck another one and there she was beside a beautiful Christmas tree, bigger and with more decorations than the one she'd seen last Christmas through the glass doors of a rich merchant's house. Thousands of candles were burning in its green branches with an array of coloured pictures like the ones you could see in the print-shop windows. The little one stretched both her hands towards them — and out went the match. But the Christmas lights rose up higher and higher so that they looked to her like stars and one of them fell, leaving a long streak in the heavens.

"Now someone's died," said the little one, for her old grandmother — the only person who'd ever been kind to her and had now died herself — she always used to say that when a star fell it was a soul going up to God.

She struck another match against the wall and there, in the light that shone from it, stood her old grandmother.

"Oh, grandma," cried the little one, "take me with you. I know you'll go when the

She took the little girl into her arms and together they flew high

match burns out, just like the stove, and the gorgeous goose, and the big, wonderful Christmas tree!" and she wildly struck all the rest of the matches in her bundle to try to hold on to her grandmother. And the matches burned with a light that was brighter than the day. Never before had her grandmother been so strong and so beautiful. She took the little girl into her arms and together they flew high — oh so high — in brightness and bliss. There was no cold any more, no hunger, no anguish — they were with God.

When the chill morning came, there by the corner of the house sat the little match girl, rosy-cheeked and smiling — frozen dead on the last night of the old year. New Year's Day dawned over her body, sitting there among the burnt-out bundle of matches. "She was trying to warm herself," said everyone, but nobody knew the beauty she had seen or the glory with which she and her grandmother had entered the joy of the New Year.

THE OLD HOUSE

Just down the street there used to be an old, old house. It had been there nearly three-hundred years — you could tell that because on one of its beams they'd carved a date, all decorated with tulips and winding hop-plants. There were whole verses spelt out in old-fashioned language, and on the beams over the windows leering gargoyle faces had been carved. One storey stuck out a good way over the one below and just under the roof there was a lead spout like a dragon's head. Rain water was meant to come out of its mouth, but it came out of its stomach instead because there was a hole in the gutter.

All the other houses in the street were nice and new with stuccoed walls and big windows — you could see straight away that they didn't want anything to do with the old house. "How long have we got to put up with that tumbledown wreck making a sight of the whole street?" they said to themselves. "That gable sticks out so far that you can't see from our windows what's going on down at the corner. And those front steps are so broad they might do for a castle, and so high you'd think they were for a church tower — and look at the iron railings like something round somebody's family grave, with great brass knobs on. It's just vulgar."

Just across the street there was one of these nice, neat houses which thought the same as the rest, but sitting in its window was a little boy, bright-eyed and rosy-cheeked, and he was very fond of the old house, whether seeing it in sunshine or by the light of the moon. And when he looked over at its walls, where the plaster had fallen off he could imagine all sorts of strange pictures — what the street had looked like in earlier times with its steps, its bay windows and its pointed gables. He could see soldiers with halberds and water-spouts that looked like dragons and basilisks.

It really was a house worth looking at and in it there lived an old man who went about in corduroy knee breeches, wore a coat with big brass buttons and had a wig which you could see really was a wig. Every morning another old chap would come to do some tidying up and run errands, but otherwise the old man in the corduroy breeches was all by himself in the old house. Now and then he'd come and look out of the window and the little boy would nod at him and the old man would nod back, so first they were just acquaintances, and then they were friends, all without ever saying a word to each other — such a thing didn't really matter.

The little boy heard his father and mother say, "That old man over there, he's pretty well off, y'know, but he must be shocking lonely."

Next Sunday, the little boy wrapped something in a piece of paper, went down to the front door, and when the old servant chap came by he said to him, "Please sir, could you give this to the old man over there from me? I've got two tin soldiers here and this is one of them and I'd like him to have it. He must be shocking lonely."

And the old chap looked very pleased and he nodded and took the tin soldier over to the old house. Then, soon after that a message came over inviting the little boy himself to pay a visit and, since his mother and father said he could, off he went to the old house.

The brass knobs on the railings up the front steps shone more brightly than ever, you might think they'd been specially polished for the visit. And some of the carved trumpeters (for there were carved trumpeters standing in the carved tulips on the front door) blew with all their might, their cheeks puffed out much rounder than ever before. Yes — they blew "*Tan-tan-tarrar* — the little boy is coming — *tan-tan-tarra*" — and then the door was opened. The whole hallway was hung with portraits of knights in armour, which clanked, and ladies in silk dresses, which rustled. Then they came to a staircase which went a great way up and a little way down — and then you were on a balcony which was really in a bad way, with big holes and long cracks in it, but grass and plants were growing all over the place and the whole balcony, the courtyard and the walls were so covered in greenery that it looked like a garden, but it wasn't much more than a balcony. Over there were some old flowerpots with faces on them with asses' ears and flowers growing any way they wanted. Pinks were in one of them with their green sprouts crowding up, shoot upon shoot, as if they were saying, "Here I am, caressed by the air, kissed by the sun, and promised 'a little flower for Sunday – a little flower for Sunday'!"

And then they came to a room where the walls were panelled with pigskin, all stamped with golden flowers:

Flowers fade fast
But pigskin will last,

said the walls.

And there were some armchairs, high-backed, carved, and with arms at both sides, "Sit you down; sit you down!", said one of them, and then, "Oooer! That gives me a wrench in the innards. Now I'm in for some gout like the old cupboard. Gout in me back, oooer!"

And so the little boy came to the room with the bay window where the old man sat.

"Thank you very much for the tin soldier, my young friend," said the old man, "and thank you for coming over to see me."

"Thanks, thanks!", or else, "Crack, crack!" said all the furniture. There was so much of it that the pieces got in each other's way trying to see the little boy. And in the centre of the wall there hung the portrait of a beautiful lady, young, smiling, but dressed like they were in the old days with powder in her hair and a dress with a bustle at the back. She didn't say either "thanks" or "crack" but looked down on the little boy with kind eyes so that he straight away said to the old man, "Where did she come from?"

"From the dealer over the way," said the old man. "Oh, there are so many pictures there and nobody recognises them or knows anything about them for they're all dead and buried. But I knew this lady in the old days, even though she's been gone now fifty years or more." And beneath the portrait, under glass, there was a nosegay of withered flowers, which looked so old that they too might have been there for fifty years. And the pendulum of the big clock went back and forth, and the hands went round and round, and everything in the room got that much older, but you wouldn't

"I can't stand it!" said the tin soldier

have noticed it.

"They say at home that you're shocking lonely," said the little boy.

"Oh," said he, "old thoughts, with all that they carry, come and visit me, and now you've come too. I'm very blessed." And he took down from the shelf a picture book showing great long cavalcades such as you never see these days: soldiers all looking like the jack of clubs and people waving flags. The tailors had shears on their flags held by a couple of lions; the shoemakers' one didn't have boots on it but an eagle with two heads (being shoemakers they had to be able to say of everything, "That makes a pair"). Yes indeed, that was some picture book.

And the old man went into a next door room to get jam and apples and nuts — oh, it was all pretty terrific over in the old house.

"I can't stand it!" said the tin soldier, who was standing on a chest of drawers, to the little boy. "It's so lonely here, so boring. Oh, no — once you've lived in a family you can't do with this place. I can't stand it. Every day is so long, and every evening is even longer. It's not like it was over the way, where your dad and mum were chatting so cheerfully all the time and you and the other kids liked to kick up such a din. Oh no — it's lonely with this old bloke. Do you think any one comes to give him a kiss — give him a smile — give him a Christmas tree? All he's going to get is a coffin. I can't stand it here."

"You mustn't take it so hard," said the little boy, "it all seems to me to be very beautiful with all the old thoughts and all that they carry coming to see him."

"Well I don't see them," said the tin soldier. "I don't know what he's on about. I can't stand it."

"Well you've got to," said the little boy. And the old man came in with his kindly face and the jam and the apples and the nuts, and the little boy thought no more about the tin soldier.

Happy and delighted, the little boy went home. Weeks went by, days went by, there was much nodding to and from the old house, and then the little boy went back there again. The carved trumpeters blew, "*Tan-tan-tarra!* Here comes the little boy — *tan-tan-tarra!*" The knights in the pictures rattled their swords and armour, the silken dresses rustled, the pigskin panels muttered, and the armchairs — "ow!" — got gout in their backs. It was all exactly the same as the first time since one day, or even one hour, was just like another over there.

"I can't stand it!" said the tin soldier. "I've been weeping tin tears. It's so boring here. I'd sooner go off to war and lose my arms and legs – that would be a change. I can't stand it. Now, yes, I know all about old thoughts coming to see me with all they carry. I've had visits from some of mine and I've decided they're not up to much in the long run. I was all for jumping off this chest of drawers. I saw everything going on in your house as clearly as if I'd been there. It was a usual Sunday morning. All you children were standing round the table singing your morning hymn – standing there very pious with your folded hands, and your dad and mum just as solemn. Then the door opens and your little sister Maria is brought in – not yet two years old – and always dancing when she hears music and singing, no matter what. She wasn't meant to, but she started dancing and couldn't get the rhythm because the tune was too slow. First she stood on one leg, with her head bent over, and then on the other leg with her head bent over, but it wouldn't do. You all stood round, taking it very serious, but me? I was laughing so much inside that I fell off the table and got a bruise that's still there – I really shouldn't have been laughing. So I can see it all again and everything that's happened to me, so I suppose those are all the old thoughts, paying their visit. Tell me though, do you still sing on Sundays? Tell me something about little Maria, and how goes my old comrade, the other tin soldier, he's the lucky one. Me? I can't stand it."

"You've been given away," said the little boy. "You've got to stay here. Don't you see?" And the old man came in with a drawer full of all sorts of things to look at: packets of crayons, jars of perfume, old cards, much bigger and covered in gilt such as you never see today. More big drawers were opened and the harpsichord was opened with landscapes painted inside its lid and a croaky voice when the old man played it. He hummed a tune. "Yes," he said, "she could sing that." He nodded towards the portrait that he had bought at the dealer's, and his eyes gleamed.

"I'm off to the wars – off to the wars!" shouted the tin soldier as loudly as he could and threw himself on to the floor.

But where had he gone to? The old man hunted, the little boy hunted, but he'd gone and he stayed gone. "I'll find him one of these days," said the old man, but he never did. The floor was so warped and rotten that the tin soldier had fallen through a crack and found himself in an open grave.

And the day went by and the little boy went home. And the weeks went by one after another. The windows frosted up and the little boy had to sit and breathe on them to make a peephole to see across to the old house. The snow blew into all the curlicues and the carved lettering and covered the front steps as though there was no one at home and indeed, there was no one at home. The old man had died.

That evening a carriage stopped outside and the old man was borne into it in his coffin and driven off to a family vault in the country. He was carried away but with never a mourner to follow, for all his friends were dead. But the little boy kissed his fingers to the coffin as it was driven away.

A few days later they had an auction at the old house and the little boy saw from the window how everything went: the ancient knights and the ancient ladies, the flowerpots with their long ears, and the old chairs and cupboards. Some things went here, some there. Her portrait, which he'd found at the dealer's, went back to the dealer's and stayed hanging there, for no one knew who she was and no one bothered any more with old pictures.

In the spring, they pulled down the house itself because everyone said it was a wreck. Standing in the street you could see into the room with the pigskin panelling which was all tattered and torn and the greenery on the balcony ran wildly over its tottering beams. So they got rid of it all quick.

"That's better!" said the houses all around.

And they built a handsome house there with big windows and white stuccoed walls, and in front, where the old house had stuck out, they planted a little garden and up by the neighbours' wall there spread the tendrils of a wild vine. In front of this garden there were big iron railings with a railed gate that looked very stately, for people to stand by and look in. Sparrows by the dozen clustered among the vine branches, gossiping away as best they could, but not about the old house because they couldn't remember it. Indeed, so many years had passed that the little boy had grown up to be a man — yes, a man of parts, the pride of his old parents. He'd just got married and had moved with his young bride into the new house with the garden and here he was, standing beside her, while she planted a wild flower that she had found and had thought very pretty. She planted it with her small hand and patted the earth round it with her fingers. Ow! — What was that? She'd pricked herself. Something sharp was sticking up in the soft earth.

And it was — believe it or not — the tin soldier, the one lost upstairs by the old man. He'd tumbled and rumbled amongst all the planks and gravel only to end up lying for many a long year here in the earth.

And the young bride dried the soldier, first with a green leaf and then with her lacy handkerchief, scented with perfume. To the tin soldier it seemed like the end of a long winter's hibernation.

"Let's have a look at him," said the young man, smiling and shaking his head. "Surely, surely, he can't be the same, but he reminds me of something that happened with a tin soldier that I had when I was a little boy." And he told his bride about the old house and the old man and the tin soldier that he'd sent over because he thought he was so shocking lonely. And he told it so exactly, just as it happened, that he brought tears to the eyes of his young bride because of the old house and the old man.

"Well, it could be the same tin soldier," she said, "I'll look after him and remember everything you've told me. You must show me the old man's grave."

"I don't know where it is," said her husband, "nobody knows where it is. All his friends were dead; no one was with him, and I was only a little boy."

"Yes, he must have been shocking lonely," she said.

"Shocking lonely!" said the tin soldier. "But it's grand not to be forgotten."

"Grand!" said somebody just by them, but no one except the tin soldier saw that it was a rag of the old pigskin panelling. It had lost all its gilt and looked like a bit of wet earth but it had its own opinions and remarked:

Gilding fades fast,
But pigskin will last.

But the tin soldier didn't believe it.

THE DUNG BEETLE

The Emperor's horse was being given gold horseshoes – gold horseshoes! – one for each hoof.

So why on earth was he getting gold horseshoes?

Oh, he was the most beautiful creature – delicate legs, wise eyes, and a mane that hung down like a silken veil over his neck. He'd carried his master through shell-smoke and the rain of bullets, bullets whistling and singing around them; he'd bitten, he'd kicked, he'd battled against the advancing enemy. Carrying his Emperor he'd sprung over the fallen horse of his enemy, saved the red gold of his Emperor's crown, saved his Emperor's life (worth more than any red gold). And so the Emperor's horse was in the forge being given gold horseshoes – gold horseshoes! – one for each hoof.

But then the dung beetle crept out.

"First the big ones, then the little ones," said he, "not that size makes any difference," and he stuck out a little leg towards the blacksmith.

"What d'you want?" asked the smith.

"Gold shoes, of course," said the dung beetle.

"Use your brains," said the smith, "you mean to say you want gold shoes as well?"

"Gold shoes," said the dung beetle. "Aren't I as good as that great beast over there, getting waited on by everyone, brushed and fussed over and given all that food and drink? Aren't I in the Emperor's stable too?"

"But don't you get why the horse has been given these gold shoes?" asked the smith.

"Get it? What I get is that you despise me," said the dung beetle. "It's a downright insult — so I'm clearing out to have a look at the great wide world."

"Be off with you then," said the smith.

"You great lout!" said the dung beetle, and he went out, flew a little way and there he was in a pretty little flower garden, all sweet with roses and lavender.

"It's nice here, isn't it?" said one of the little ladybirds, fluttering her tiny red shield-like wings with their black spots on. "How sweet it all smells, how charming."

"I'm used to better than this," said the dung beetle. "D'you call this charming? Why, it's not even got a dung-heap."

So he went on a bit into the shade of a big gilliflower. There was a caterpillar creeping about.

"Isn't the world just beautiful?" said the caterpillar. "The sun's so warm, everything's so very enjoyable. And when I go to sleep and die, as they say I will, then I'll wake up as a butterfly."

"Well how stuck up is that?" said the dung beetle. "The likes of you flying about like a butterfly! I'm from the Emperor's stable, but nobody there — not even the Emperor's favourite horse, who's got my cast-off golden shoes — has such ideas. Wings? Fly? Why, I can do that now!" And off flew the dung beetle. "I don't really want to be cross, but I *am* cross."

So he dumped himself down on a big patch of grass, lay there for a bit and then fell asleep.

And then what? Rain! A great downpour! The dung beetle woke up soaked and tried to burrow into the earth, but he couldn't. He wallowed around, trying to swim on his front then his back — there was no hope of flying and he wondered if he'd get out of the place alive. There was nothing for it but to lie where he was lying, so there he lay.

The rain lifted a bit and the dung beetle blinked the water out of his eyes and spotted something white ahead, some linen put out to bleach. He crawled up to it and crept into one of its damp folds. It was hardly like his warm heap in the stable but there was nothing better to be had so he stayed there the whole day and the whole

"Gold shoes, of course," said the dung beetle

night as well, since it just went on raining. Next morning the dung beetle crawled out, furious at the lousy weather.

There were a couple of frogs sitting on the linen, their bright eyes glittering with pleasure. "What wonderful weather!" said one of them. "How very refreshing! And this linen here collects up the water so well that it gets my back legs all of a quiver; I could almost swim."

"I'd just like to know," said the other one, "if the swallow, for all his flying around in one country or another, has ever found a better climate than what we've got here. All drizzly and damp – why, it's like lying in a good, wet ditch. If you don't care for this, you can hardly care for the land you live in."

"Were you ever in the Emperor's stables?" asked the dung beetle. "The wet there is all warm and spicy. That's what suits me; that's my weather, but I can't carry it around with me on my travels. Haven't you got a muck-heap in this garden where a person of quality like me can take up residence and make himself at home?" But the frogs didn't know what he was talking about, and, what's more, didn't want to know.

"I never ask twice," said the dung beetle, having asked three times without getting an answer.

So he went on a bit and found a broken flowerpot. It certainly shouldn't have been there but it offered some shelter. Several families of earwigs were living there, not taking up much house-room but they were all for mucking in together. The ladies were especially endowed with motherly pride, each thinking her own offspring the cleverest and the most gifted of the lot. "Our son," said one mother, "has got himself engaged, the dear little innocent! His great aim is to creep into a priest's ear. Boys will be boys, you know, however lovable, but since he's engaged that should keep him out of mischief. Oh, what a delight he is to his mother."

"Our son," said another proud mama, "was up to his games as soon as he got out of the egg, running his little horns off – such a joy for his mother, don't you think so, Mr Dung Beetle?" (For she recognised the stranger from his shape.)

"Quite right the two of you," said the dung beetle, so they invited him in so long as he could find room in the broken pot.

"Now you must see my little earwig," said a third mother and then a fourth. "Aren't they just the most delightful children, and so funny. They're never naughty except when they have the collywobbles, but that's only to be expected at their age."

And so all the mothers rattled on about their children and the children rattled on too and used the little nippers that they have in their tails to tweak the dung beetle's moustache.

"Oh, they can't keep off anything, the little rogues," said all these mothers, gushing with maternal pride. But the dung beetle was bored by it all and asked if there happened to be a dung heap anywhere around.

"Ooh, that's a world away on the other side of the ditch," said the earwigs, "such a way off that I hope to goodness none of my little ones go off there. It'd be the death of me."

"Well, I'll try to get there," said the dung beetle and he went off without saying goodbye – a very courteous thing to do, to be sure.

Over by the ditch he met several acquaintances, all of them dung beetles.

"Here's home," they said, "it's a comfy place – the fat of the land – come on down. You've done some travelling."

"I surely have," said the dung beetle. "I had to shelter in some linen from the rain and all that cleanliness doesn't agree with me. What's more, I've got rheumatism in my wings from standing in a draught by a broken flowerpot. I must say, it's very cheering to be back among friends."

"Have you come from a compost heap then?" asked the eldest.

"Better than that," said the dung beetle. "I've come from the Emperor's stable where I was born with golden shoes on my feet. I'm travelling on a secret mission. Don't ask about it, my lips are sealed." So the dung beetle stepped down into the rich mud and there sat three lady dung beetles tittering because they didn't know what to say.

"They're not spoken for," said their mother and they tittered again, this time out of embarrassment.

"I've not seen such beauties even in the Emperor's stable," said our much-travelled dung beetle.

"Don't you spoil my little girls – and don't go talking to them unless you've got proper intentions. Oh, but I see you have! I give you my blessing."

"Whoopee!" said everyone, and the dung beetle was engaged. Engaged first, then married – there was no point in hanging around.

The next day passed very pleasantly. The one after that much the same. But the third day there was the question of feeding the wife and – who knows? – some little ones too.

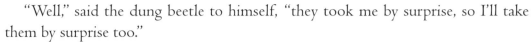

"Well," said the dung beetle to himself, "they took me by surprise, so I'll take them by surprise too."

And so he did. He went off – went off for a whole day, went off for a whole night, and his wife sat there like a widow. The other dung beetles thought that he was a right vagabond, taking up with their family like that, and now his bride was just a burden to them.

"Well she'll just have to be a virgin again and sit with the other girls," said her mother, "and a plague on the wretch who deserted her." Meanwhile the dung beetle journeyed on and sailed across the bottom of the ditch on a cabbage leaf.

In the morning two chaps spotted the dung beetle, took him up, rolled him and turned him about, and both of them – especially the boy – discussed him in learned terms: "'*Allah seeth the black beetle in the black stone in the black rock*.' Doesn't it say that in the Koran?" he asked, and then translated the dung beetle's name into Latin and launched into an account of his nature and genus. The older scholar voted against taking him home – "We've got specimens just as good back there," he said – and that seemed uncivil to the dung beetle so he took off out of his hand and flew away. Since his wings were now dry, he was able to get comfortably to a greenhouse where he slipped in through an open shutter and buried himself in some nice fresh manure.

"Just the place to stay," he said.

Soon he fell asleep and dreamed that the Emperor's horse had died and that he, Mr Dung beetle, was to have the golden shoes with a promise of two more. That was very satisfying and the dung beetle woke up, crept out, and looked around him. What a splendid greenhouse it was! Great palm trees towered up, seemingly transparent in the sunshine, while under them sprang up an abundance of green and shining flowers: red as gold, yellow as amber, white as new-fallen snow.

"A matchless flower show! How delicious they'll be when they've rotted down," said the dung beetle. "It's like a great larder; there must be some of my relations here. I'll have a look round for someone to talk to. Only someone worthwhile, mind – I have my pride and I'm proud to have it." So he wandered off, thinking of his dream of the dead horse and the golden shoes he had inherited.

Then suddenly a hand seized the dung beetle, rolling and turning him round again.

The gardener's little boy and a chum of his had come into the greenhouse, spotted the dung beetle and decided to have some fun with him. He was wrapped in a vine leaf, stuck in the boy's all-too-warm trouser pocket, where he skittered and skuttered only to be manhandled some more. They quickly went down to a big lake at the bottom of the garden. Here the dung beetle was put into a broken old wooden shoe without an instep. A little stick did for a mast and the dung beetle was tied to it with a thread of wool. Now he was skipper of the ship, off for a sail.

It was a pretty big lake and seemed like an ocean to the dung beetle. He was so astonished that he fell on to his back and waved his legs in the air.

The wooden shoe sailed into a current but whenever it got too far from the shore one of the boys would roll up his trousers and wade in to bring it back to land. But just as it set out again there was a shout for the boys – a pretty sharp shout – and they scampered off, leaving the wooden shoe no longer a boat but just a wooden shoe. It drifted further and further from land, giving the dung beetle the horrors since he was still tied fast to the mast.

Then a fly paid him a visit.

"We're having grand weather now," said the fly. "I'll hang around a bit here, get a bit of sunshine. You look very comfortable."

"Well that's a very bright remark. Can't you see I'm tethered here?"

"Well I'm not," said the fly, and flew away.

"Now I see what sort of a world it is," said the dung beetle. "It's a lousy world and I'm the only decent creature in it. First they won't give me golden shoes, then I have to lie down in wet linen, stand in a draught and have a wife foisted on to me. And no sooner do I manage a quick getaway from that, seeing how the world wags and me along with it, than those whelpish kids put me at the mercy of the wild ocean. And all the time the Emperor's horse is prancing around in his golden shoes. That's what gets to me most, but there's no sympathy to be had in this world. My busy life has been full of interest, but what's the good of that when nobody knows about it? And they don't deserve to know about it, otherwise they'd have given me those golden shoes in the Emperor's stable when his favourite horse stretched out his legs to get them. If I'd had those shoes I'd be an honour to the stable; now I'm lost to them and lost to the world – done for."

But not done for, for along came a boat with some young girls in it.

"Look, there's a wooden shoe floating along," said one of them.

"And there's a little animal tied to it," said another.

And they came alongside the wooden shoe, fished it out, and one of the girls took out some little scissors, clipped away the wool without hurting the dung beetle, and then set him down in the grass once they'd landed.

"Creep, little one, creep! Fly, fly if you can," she said. "Freedom's a grand thing."

And the dung beetle flew — *whizz* — into the open window of a big building and he sank down wearily into the fine, soft, long mane of the Emperor's favourite horse, there in the stable where he and the dung beetle had their home. He clung fast to the mane and buzzed away to himself, "Here I am, sitting on the Emperor's favourite horse — just like a knight. What a thing to say! Why, it's all plain to me now — all clear and correct." 'Don't you get why the horse has golden shoes?' said that smith back then. Well, now it's plain. The horse has the golden shoes on my account, as I am to be his appointed knight."

And the dung beetle cheered up at once.

"Ah, travelling's good for the brains," he said.

The sun shone down on him, shone very beautifully. "The world's not so bad after all," said the dung beetle, "but you've got to know how to take it. Now I'll go down to the other beetles and let them know how much has been done for me. I'll let them know all the pleasures I've enjoyed on my foreign travels and say that I'm home now till the horse wears out his golden shoes."

THE SNOWMAN

"I'm all of a crackle inside with this scrumptious cold!" said the snowman. "The wind really blows a bit of life into you! And how that glowing thing glowers!" (He meant the sun, which was just about to set.) "He'll not make me blink; I can still keep hold of my bits and pieces."

He was talking about two big, triangular bits of tile, which were his eyes; his mouth was part of an old rake, so that he'd got teeth. He'd been born to the sound of boys cheering and greeted with the jingle of sleigh-bells and the cracking of whips.

The sun set. The full moon came up, big and round, shining white and beautiful in the darkening air. "Here he comes again from the other side," said the snowman. (He thought it was the sun come up again.) "I saw him. Off with all his glowering! Now he can hang up there and shine away so that I can see myself. If only I knew how people moved and got about! I'd very much like to get about myself. If I could, I'd go down there and slide on the ice like I saw the boys doing, but I don't know how to run."

"*Grroff! Grroff!*" barked the old watchdog. He was a bit hoarse, which had happened since the days when he'd been a house dog and lain by the fire. "The sun'll teach you

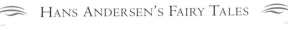

how to run! I saw that with the chap who was here before you – and with the chap before him. *Grroff! Grroff!* Everybody *grroff!*"

"Now then, friend, I don't know what you're talking about!" said the snowman. "Him up there teach me to run?" (He meant the moon.) "Oh, yes! He was running himself right enough last time I looked at him; now he's sneaking back from the other side."

"You're stupid," said the watchdog, "but then you've only just been slapped together! What you're looking at now is called the moon; the sun was the one before. He'll come again tomorrow morning and he'll teach you to run down there into the ditch by the wall. We're in for a change of weather – I can tell because I get pains in my left back leg. We're in for a shift of weather."

"I don't know what he's talking about at all," said the snowman, "but I've got an idea that it's not something nice. That thing that glowered and then disappeared, that he called the sun, he's certainly no friend of mine – I can feel it in my bones."

"*Grroff! Grroff!*" barked the watchdog, turned himself round three times, and lay down in the kennel to go to sleep.

And a change in the weather really did come. Towards morning there was a thick, clammy mist over everything; then later the wind got up – icy cold – the frost gripped everything. But what a sight it was when the sun came up! All the trees and bushes were covered with hoar frost, like a whole forest of white coral, where all the twigs bloomed with glittering white flames. The delicate tracery of branches that you can't see in summer because of all the leaves now showed up clearly. It was like lace, and so gleaming white, with white lights glimmering from every twig. The birch tree lifted its branches in the wind, live, like the trees in summer it was wonderfully beautiful! And when the sun shone down everything sparkled as if it was powdered with a dust of diamonds, with big diamonds glinting in the drifts of snow. You'd think that countless little lights were burning, whiter than the white snow.

"That is wonderfully beautiful," said a young girl, coming out into the garden with a young man and standing next to the snowman, looking at the glittering trees. "You wouldn't see it so beautiful, even in summer!" she said and her eyes sparkled.

"And you won't have a fellow like this here then," said the young man, and he pointed to the snowman. "He's splendid."

The young girl laughed, nodded at the snowman and danced off with her friend over the snow, which crunched under her as though she was walking on starch.

"Who were those two?" the snowman asked the watchdog. "You've been on this farm longer than I have, do you know 'em?"

"Of course I do!" said the watchdog. "She's patted me and he's given me bones. I don't bite them."

"But what are they up to here?" asked the snowman.

"Courrrr—, courrrr—, courting!" said the watchdog. "They'll be moving into the same kennel and gnawing bones together. *Grroff! Grroff!*"

"And are those two as important as you and me?" asked the snowman.

"They belong to the guvnor," said the watchdog. "Really, people born yesterday are an ignorant lot and you're one of 'em! As for me – I've got age and wisdom; I know everything that's going on at this farm! And what's more, I know a time when I wasn't chained up out here in the cold. *Grroff! Grroff!*"

"The cold's very nice," said the snowman. "But come on, tell me all about it – only don't keep rattling your chain, it gives me the willies inside."

"*Grroff! Grroff!*" barked the watchdog. "I was young once. 'Oh isn't he a sweet little thing,' they used to say, and I lay in a velvet chair up there in the farmhouse, lay in the guvnor's lap. They used to kiss my nose and wipe my paws with an embroidered handkerchief and it was all 'prettykins' and 'dear little woofums'. But then I got too big for them, so they gave me to the housekeeper and I had to live in the basement! You can see where it was from where you're standing; you can see down into the room where *I* was guvnor – because that's what I was at the housekeeper's. It may have been a smaller place than upstairs, but I was more comfy, and I wasn't pulled around and slobbered over by the children like upstairs. The food was just as good as before, and there was more of it! I had my own cushion, and there was a stove that was the best place in the world at times like this. I used to creep down under it so that I got black all over. Oh – I still dream about that stove. *Grroff! Grroff!*"

"Do stoves look as nice as all that?" asked the snowman. "Like me?"

"Like the opposite of you! It's coal-black – it's got a long neck with a brass collar – and it eats firewood so that flames come out of its mouth. If you get down beside it or, better still, under it, then it's the most comfortable place in the world! You can see it through the window from where you're standing."

And the snowman looked, and sure enough he saw a black, polished thing with a brass collar and flames flickering down below. The snowman came over all peculiar;

The snowman stood there for the whole day, looking through the window

he had a strange feeling that he couldn't put a name to; it wasn't anything he knew about – but most people will know it, provided they're not snowmen.

"And why did you leave her?" asked the snowman. (He felt that the stove must be some sort of woman.) "How could you leave such a lovely place?"

"I'd no choice," said the watchdog. "They threw me out and chained me up here. I'd bitten the youngest young master in the leg because he pinched the bone that I was gnawing. Well – 'bone for bone', says I, but they didn't like it, and from then on I've been on this chain, and I've lost my nice voice. Just hear how hoarse I am: *Grroff! Grroff!* That's the finish of it."

But the snowman wasn't listening. He kept on looking into the housekeeper's room in the cellar where the stove stood on its four iron legs, the same height as the snowman himself.

"Everything's scrunching down inside me," he said. "Shall I ever get in there? It's an innocent enough wish, and innocent wishes must surely be granted. It's my highest wish, my only wish, and it really wouldn't be fair for it not to be granted. I must get in there, I must get beside her, even if I have to break a window."

"You'll never get in," said the watchdog, "and if you did reach the stove then you'd soon get off – *grroff! Grroff!*"

"I'm as good as off," said the snowman, "I think I'm breaking up."

The snowman stood there for the whole day, looking through the window. As the light faded the room looked even more inviting. A gentle light came from the stove, not like the moon or the sun – no – it was like the light of a stove when it's got something inside it. When they opened its door flames leapt out as they always did. It made the snowman's white face red with blushes which went on half-way down his body.

"I can't take it," he said. "How beautiful she is with her tongue out!"

It was a long, long night – but not for the snowman. He was lost in his own beautiful thoughts and freezing till he crackled.

In the morning the cellar windows were frozen over with the most beautiful flowers of ice that any snowman could wish for – but they hid the stove. The ice wouldn't melt on the panes, so he couldn't see her. Everything crackled and crunched; it was just the kind of frosty weather that a snowman should enjoy – but he didn't enjoy it; he could – and really should – have felt so light-hearted – but he wasn't light-hearted.

He was love sick for the stove.

"That's a nasty complaint for a snowman," said the watchdog. "Mind you, I've had it myself, but I got over it. *Grroff! Grroff!* Now we'll get a shift in the weather."

And the weather did shift; it began to thaw. And the more the weather thawed, the more the snowman thawed too. But he didn't say anything; he didn't grizzle – and that's a sure sign...

One morning he collapsed. Where he stood something stuck up in the air like the handle of a broom, and that's what the boys had built him round.

"Now I can see why he was love sick," said the watchdog. "The snowman had a stove rake in his body, and that's what was making him so spoony – but now he's got over it. *Grroff! Grroff!*"

And soon they'd got over the weather too.

"*Grroff! Grroff!*" barked the watchdog – but the little girls on the farm sang:

"Primrose, primrose
Pretty face!
Willow, willow
Woolly lace!
Lark and cuckoo
Come and sing,
February
Heralds spring.
Whistle, whistle
Call – call –
Come the sunshine
Over all."

And nobody thought about the snowman.

THE SNOW QUEEN
AN ADVENTURE IN SEVEN STORIES

FIRST STORY
WHICH TELLS OF THE MIRROR AND THE SPLINTERS

Come on now — look! We're going to begin. And when we get to the end of this story we shall know more than we do now, because here's a wicked troll — really — one of the nastiest, and that's the Devil himself.

One day he was in a very good mood, because he'd made a mirror which had this strange power, that whenever anything good or pretty was reflected in it, it shrank down almost to nothing, while whatever was paltry or ugly filled the whole glass and looked even worse than it was. The most beautiful landscapes looked like boiled spinach, and the very best people turned hideous or stood on their heads with their stomachs all gone. Faces were so twisted about that no one would know them, and if you'd got a single freckle then you'd find that it spread out right over your nose and your mouth. ("That was really good fun," said the Devil.) Now if anyone had a good or saintly thought, then the mirror would grin and the old devil-troll would have to laugh at his artistic invention. Everyone who went to the troll-school (for he kept a school for trolls) spread the word that it was altogether a miracle: now, they said, for the first time you could see what the world and the people in it really looked like. They ran around with the mirror and eventually there wasn't a single country or a single person who hadn't been bent about in it. And now they were going to fly up to heaven as well, to make fools of the angels and the good Lord himself. The higher they flew with the mirror, the more widely it grinned and they could scarcely hang on to it. Higher and higher they flew, nearer to God and the angels; then the mirror shook so frightfully with all its grinning that it sprang out of their hands and fell down to Earth, where it broke into a hundred million billion bits – or even more – and then it made much worse trouble than before; for some of the bits were hardly as big as a grain of sand and these flew about across the whole wide world, and when they got into people's eyes they stuck there so that those people saw everything twisted, or got a sharp eye for finding fault with things – for every little splinter of the mirror possessed the same powers as the whole mirror had done. Some people even got a little piece of glass in their hearts, and that was really horrible because then their hearts were like blocks of ice. Some bits of the mirror were so big that they were made into window panes, but it didn't do to look at your friends through panes of glass like that. Other bits were put into spectacles, and then it was pretty awful if people put on such spectacles to try to see if everything was right and just. The Wicked One was so tickled by all this that he laughed till his belly shook.

But, outside, little pieces of glass still flew round in the air. Now let's hear about them!

SECOND STORY
WHICH TELLS OF A LITTLE BOY AND A LITTLE GIRL

In the big city where there are so many houses and so many people that there isn't room for everyone to have a garden, so that most people have to make do with flowers in a flowerpot, there were two poor children, and they had a garden that was a bit bigger than a flowerpot. They weren't brother and sister, but they were just as fond of each other as if they had been. Their parents lived opposite each other, way up in a couple of attics, and where the roof from one house joined that of its neighbour and a flat gulley ran along between the two roofs, there each of the houses had a little window. You'd only to step over the gulley and you could get from one window to the other.

Outside, their parents each had a big wooden box, where they grew the kitchen herbs which they needed, and also a little rose tree; there was one in each box and they grew a treat. Now the parents had the idea of putting these boxes longways over the gulley so that they stretched from one window to the other and looked for all the world like two banks of flowers. Sweetpeas trailed down over the sides of the boxes and the rose trees stretched out their long branches, wreathed them round the windows, tangled them with each other, so that it all looked like a triumphal arch made of green leaves and flowers. And, since the boxes were very high up and the children knew that they mustn't climb on them, they were often allowed to step out to see one another, sit on their little stools under the roses and play wonderful games together.

In winter this sort of fun had to stop as the windows were often completely covered with frost. But then they'd warm copper coins on the stove and put the hot pennies on the frozen panes so that they'd get a lovely round, round peephole, and behind it you'd see from each window a twinkling, smiling eye – the little boy, and the little girl. He was Kay and she was Gerda. In summer they could meet each other with just one jump; in winter they first had to go down a lot of stairs then up a lot of stairs, with the snow tumbling down outside.

"Those are the white bees swarming," said Old Granny.

"And have they got a queen bee?" asked the little boy, because he knew that real bees had one.

"That they have!" said Granny. "She's flying there where the swarm's thickest! She's the biggest one of all, and she never rests quiet on the earth but flies up again to the dark sky. Many a winter's night she flies back to the streets in the town and peeps in at the windows, and then they freeze over so that they look as though they're covered with flowers."

"Yes – yes – I've seen that," said the two children, so they knew it was true.

"Can the Snow Queen come in here?" asked the little girl.

"Just let her try," said the boy. "I'll put her on the hot stove and melt her."

But Old Granny stroked his hair and told them some more stories.

That evening, when little Kay was back home and half ready for bed, he climbed up on the stool by the window and peeped through the little hole. A few snowflakes were falling outside, and one of these — the largest of them — stayed lying on the edge of one of the window boxes. This snowflake grew, bigger and bigger, till at last it turned into a maiden, dressed in the finest white gauze which was covered with millions of starry flakes. She was so delicate and beautiful — but she was ice, flashing, glittering ice — and yet she was alive. Her eyes shone like two bright stars, but there was no rest or peace in them. She nodded at the window and beckoned with her hand. The little boy was frightened and jumped down from his stool, for it was as if a huge bird flew past the window outside.

The next day there was a clear frost — and then there was a thaw — and then the spring came. The sun shone, the trees grew green, the swallows built their nests, the windows were opened again and the children sat in their little garden high up on the roof, over all the rooms and stairs and landings of the house.

How marvellously the roses bloomed that summer! The little girl had learned a hymn which had something about roses in it, and those roses made her think about her own; and she sang about them to the little boy and then he sang with her:

Little Jesus walked with us,
Little Jesus talked with us,
Down in the valley where the roses grow.

And the two of them held each other's hands, kissed the roses and gazed about in God's bright sunshine, talking to it as if the child Jesus really was there. Oh! Those were glorious summer days — everything blissful outside there among the young rose trees which never seemed to stop flowering.

Kay and Gerda were sitting looking at a picture book full of animals and flowers when, just at the moment when the clock in the big church tower struck five, Kay said, "Ow! — What's that stuck me in the heart! And now I've got something in my eye!" The little girl put her arm round his neck; he blinked his eye — no, there was nothing to be seen.

"I think it's gone," he said, but it wasn't gone. It was one of those little splinters of glass from the mirror (you remember?), that old troll-mirror — that wicked glass which made everything great and good look small and hideous while everything foul and horrible stood out as altogether respectable, and every fault could be seen at once. Poor Kay — he'd got a splinter in his heart too, and that was going to turn into a lump of ice before long. It didn't hurt any more, but it was still there.

"What're you crying for?" he asked. "Ugh, how ugly you look! There's nothing wrong with me!" And then — suddenly — he said, "Ooh! That rose! It's all wormy! And look, that one's all bent! They really are horrible roses — just like the box they're planted in!" And he kicked the box hard, and tore the roses off their stems.

"Kay, what're you doing?" cried the little girl, and when he saw what a fright he'd given her he pulled off another rose and ran back in through his own window, away from pretty little Gerda.

After that, whenever she came with her picture book he'd say that that was for babbies, and when Granny told them stories he'd always be if-ing and but-ing — indeed, when he could, he'd get behind her, put on her spectacles and copy the way she talked (he could do it just like she did and make everybody laugh), and soon he could imitate the way everyone in the whole street spoke or walked. Kay saw whatever was peculiar or silly about them and copied it, until people began to say, "He's got a sharp head on him, has that boy!" But it was all because of the bit of glass he'd got in his eye, and the bit of glass in his heart, so that he even laughed at little Gerda, who loved him with all her soul.

The games he played now were quite different from before — they were all very sensible. One winter's day, when it was snowing, he came out with a big magnifying glass, held it up to the tail of his blue coat and let the snowflakes fall on it. "Gerda — look at them through the glass," he called, and every snowflake was magnified and looked like a wonderful flower or a ten-pointed star; it was beautiful to see.

"Look! Isn't that cunning?" said Kay. "It's more interesting than real flowers. It's not got a single fault — it's completely regular — at least until it melts!"

Soon after, Kay came by with his big gloves on and his sledge on his back, and he shouted right in Gerda's ear, "They're letting me go and play in the big square with the others," and off he went.

Out there in the square the boldest boys used to tie their sledges to the farmers' carts and get pulled along behind them a fair distance. That was good fun. Then, while they were playing, a great big sledge appeared. It was painted white all over, and there was someone in it wrapped in a rough white fur and with a white rough cap on. This sledge drove round the square a couple of times, and Kay quickly tied his little sledge to the back of it and drove round too. Then it went quicker and quicker, right into the next street, and the person who drove it turned and nodded at Kay, all friendly, as though they both knew each other. Every time Kay tried to untie his little sledge this person would nod again, and Kay just stayed sitting there. And so they drove out of the city gate. Then it began to snow so heavily that the little boy couldn't see the hand on the end of his arm, and still they flew on. Then he quickly dropped the cord to get loose from the big sledge, but that was no help, his little toboggan hung on and went like the wind. So he shouted out loud, but nobody heard him, and the snow fell and the sledge flew on – now and then it would give a little jump as if it was flying over hedges and ditches. He was utterly terrified and he tried to recite "Our Father which art in Heaven...", but all he could remember was the twelve-times table.

The snowflakes were getting bigger and bigger, till they looked like great white chickens; then suddenly they parted, the big sledge stopped and its driver stood up – fur and cap made of pure snow. It was a lady, tall and slender and glittering white. It was the Snow Queen.

"We have done well," she said, "but why are you so cold? Creep here into my bearskin!" And she sat him in her own sledge, and threw the fur round him so that he seemed to sink into a snowdrift.

"Still frozen?" she asked him, and she kissed him on the forehead. Oof! That was colder than ice; that drove straight to his heart, which was already half a lump of ice; he thought he was going to die! But only for a second, then everything seemed all right and he didn't notice the cold all around him any more.

"My sledge! Don't forget my sledge!" That was the first thing he thought about, and that was tied to one of the white chickens, which flew behind them with the sledge on its back. The Snow Queen kissed Kay once more, and then he forgot little Gerda, and her granny, and everyone at home.

"No more kisses now," she said, "otherwise I'd kiss you to death!"

Kay looked at her. She was so beautiful; he didn't believe he'd ever seen a wiser or more lovely face – not all icy like the one that he'd seen beckoning to him that time outside the window. To his eyes she was perfect. He didn't feel afraid of her any more; he told her he could do mental arithmetic – with fractions, what's more – work out

They flew over forests and lakes, sea and land

the size of the country in square miles and how many people lived there; and all the time she was smiling, so that it seemed to him that he really knew nothing at all. And he looked up into the huge, huge sky, and she flew with him — flew high up on a black cloud, and when the storm winds whistled and howled it seemed as though they were singing old ballads. They flew over forests and lakes, sea and land, while below them the cold wind roared, the wolves howled, the snow glittered, and above them flew black, screaming crows. But over everything the moon shone, big and clear, and Kay looked across the long, long winter night. And when day came he slept at the Snow Queen's feet.

THIRD STORY
WHICH TELLS OF THE WISE WOMAN'S FLOWER-GARDEN

But what of little Gerda when Kay never came home? What had become of him? Nobody knew; nobody had any news. The boys only told how they'd seen him tie his sledge to a magnificent big one, which drove off down the street and out of the city gate. Nobody knew what had become of him; many tears were shed and little Gerda wept long and bitterly. Then they said he was dead — drowned in the river that ran close by the city. Oh, those were long, gloomy winter days.

Now the spring came, and warmer sunshine.

"Kay is dead and gone!" said little Gerda.

"I don't believe it!" said the sunshine.

"He is dead and gone!" she said to the swallows.

"I don't believe it!" they answered, and from then on little Gerda didn't believe it either.

"I'll put on my new red shoes," she said one morning, "the ones that Kay's never seen, and I'll go down to the river and ask for him!"

It was still very early. She kissed her old grandmother, who was still asleep, put on her red shoes and went off all by herself out of the gate and down to the river.

"Is it true that you've taken away my little playfellow? I'll give you my red shoes if you'll give him back to me again!" And it seemed to her as if the flowing water nodded at her in a strange way, so she took off her red shoes, her dearest possession, and threw both of them into the river; but they dropped in quite close to the bank and the eddies brought them straight back to her on the shore, as if the river didn't want to take her dearest possession, because it really didn't have little Kay. But she thought now that she hadn't thrown the shoes far enough out, so she climbed into a boat drawn up in the reeds, went down to the farthest end and threw the shoes again. But the boat wasn't tied up and with all this movement it slid away from the bank. She saw this and quickly tried to get back, but before she could get to the other end the boat was more than a yard off and drifted away faster than before.

Little Gerda was terrified and started to cry, but nobody heard her except the sparrows and they couldn't take her back to dry land. Instead they flew along the bank and sang as if to cheer her up, "Here we are! Here we are!" The boat drove down with the stream and little Gerda sat quite still in her stockinged feet. Her little red shoes floated after her, but they couldn't reach the boat, which went quicker and quicker.

Both the river banks were beautiful, with pretty flowers, ancient trees, and slopes dotted with sheep and cows, but not a human being to be seen. "Perhaps the river is taking me to little Kay," thought Gerda, and she felt more cheerful, stood up and, as the hours passed, watched the beautiful green banks of the river. Then, eventually, she came to a big cherry orchard where there was a little house with strange red and blue windows, a thatched roof and, outside, two wooden soldiers who presented arms to anyone sailing past.

Gerda called to them because she thought they were alive, but of course they didn't answer. Then she came quite close to them because the river carried the boat straight in towards the land.

Gerda called again, only louder, and out of the house there came an old, old woman, leaning on a crutch. She was wearing a big sun hat, painted all over with the most beautiful flowers.

"Oh, you poor little mite!" said the old woman. "How have you gotten yourself out on this big, strong river, floating off into the wide, wide world!" And the old woman went down into the water, hooked her crutch on to the boat, pulled it in to the bank and lifted little Gerda out. And Gerda was glad to be back on dry land, but she was a bit frightened of the strange, old woman.

"Come along then, and tell me who you are and how you came to be here!" said she.

And Gerda told her everything; and the old woman shook her head and said, "Hm! Hm!" When Gerda had finished telling her everything and asked if she hadn't seen little Kay, the old woman said that he'd not come that way but he might still do so; Gerda wasn't to be sad but should come and taste the cherries and look at the flowers, for these were prettier than a picture book and every one of them could tell a whole story. So she took Gerda by the hand and they went into the little house and the old woman locked the door.

The windows were all high up and their glass was red, blue and yellow; the different colours made the daylight look all queer, but on the table there were the most delicious cherries and Gerda was allowed to eat as many as she liked. And while she was eating them the old woman combed her hair with a golden comb and her hair dropped in such curls round her friendly little face and took on such a golden sheen that she looked just like a plump round rose.

"Oh, how much I've longed for such a sweet little girl as you!" said the old woman. "Now you'll just see how well the two of us will get on together!" And the more she combed little Gerda's hair the more Gerda forgot about her playmate Kay, for the old woman knew how to do witchcraft, even though she wasn't a witch — she just did it for her own enjoyment and now she really did want to keep little Gerda. Because of this, she went into the garden, stretched out her crutch over all the rose trees, and — however beautiful they were — they all sank down into the dark earth and you couldn't see where they'd been. The old woman was afraid that when Gerda saw the roses, she'd think about the ones at home and then she'd remember little Kay and run off.

Now she brought Gerda out into the flower garden — oh, how lovely it all looked and smelled! Every flower you could think of, from every season of the year, was there in fullest bloom, and not even a picture book could be more pretty and colourful. Gerda jumped for joy and played there till the sun went down behind the tall cherry trees. Then she was given a comfy bed with a red silk quilt stuffed with violets and she fell asleep and dreamed as happily as a queen on her wedding day.

The next day she played once more among the flowers in the warm sunshine — and so it went on, day after day. Gerda got to know every flower, but although there were lots of them it always seemed to her that one was missing, but which one it was she just didn't know. Then one day she was sitting looking at the old woman's sun hat with the flowers painted on it, and the prettiest one there was a rose. The old woman had forgotten to magic it away from the hat when she sent the others down into the earth — and that's the way of it if you don't keep your wits about you!

Gerda said, "What! Aren't there any roses here?" She ran about among the flower beds, looking and looking, but she couldn't find a single one. Then she sat down and cried, but her warm tears fell down just where one of the rose trees had sunk, and as those warm tears wet the earth the tree sprang up as full of flowers as when it sank. Gerda put her arms about it, kissed the roses and thought of the beautiful roses at home — and, along with them, of little Kay.

"Oh, the time I've wasted!" said the little girl. "I ought to be looking for Kay! — Do you know where he is?" she asked the roses. "Do you think he's dead and buried?"

"He's not dead," said the roses. "We've been down in the earth with all the dead people, but Kay wasn't there!"

"Thank you, thank you!" said little Gerda, and she went round all the other flowers and looked into their cups and asked, "Do you know where little Kay is?" But every flower stood there in the sunshine, dreaming its own fairy tale, its own story, and Gerda heard many a one of these, but not one about Kay.

So what did the tiger lily say?

"Listen to the drums: boom-boom! Just those two notes all the time: boom-boom! Listen to the wailing song of the widow! Listen to the shouting of the priests! — The Hindu woman stands by the funeral pyre in her long, red robe; the flames leap up around her and around her dead husband; but the Hindu woman thinks of the living one, here in the circle, him whose eyes burn hotter than the flames, him whose eyes make a fire in her heart fiercer than the flames that will soon burn her body to ashes. Can the heart's fire die with the funeral fire?"

"I don't understand that at all," said little Gerda.

"Well, that's my fairy tale," said the tiger lily.

So what does the convolvulus say?

"High above the narrow bridle path there looms an old castle. Thick ivy grows up over the old, red-stone walls, leaf upon leaf up to the balcony where a beautiful girl is standing. She bends over the balustrade and looks down the path. No rose hangs fresher on its branch than she, no apple blossom drifts lighter than she, when the breeze blows it from its tree. How richly her silken robes rustle! 'Why does he never come?'"

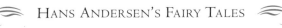

"Is that Kay you're talking about?" asked little Gerda.

"I am only saying my fairy tale, my dream," said the convolvulus.

So what does the little snowdrop say?

"There's a wooden board hanging down on ropes between the trees, and that's a swing; there are two pretty girls — dresses white as snow, long green ribbons in their hats — sitting and swinging. There's their brother, bigger than them, standing up in the swing with one arm round the rope to hold himself steady, because in one hand he's got a little bowl and in the other a clay pipe, and he's blowing bubbles. The swing swings and the bubbles fly with all their colours changing, the last one still hanging from the end of the pipe, swaying in the wind. The swing swings. A little black dog, like a bubble himself, stands up on his back legs trying to get into the swing, but it flies over him and he falls over and barks, all cross. They laugh at him and the bubbles burst. A swinging board, a drifting bubble — that's my song!"

"Well it's all very nice, and very pretty, what you say, but you make it sound so sad — and you don't mention little Kay. What do the hyacinths say?"

"There were three beautiful sisters — very fine and delicate; the first had a red dress, the second blue, and the third pure white. Hand in hand they danced beside the calm lake in the moonlight. They weren't elfin girls, they were humans. Everything there smelled so sweet, and the girls disappeared into the forest. The fragrance grew stronger; three coffins, with the beautiful maidens lying in them, came gliding from the darkness of the wood and away over the lake; glowworms flew round them, shining like little hovering lights. Are the dancing girls sleeping, or are they dead? — The scent of the flowers say death; the evening bell tolls for the dead!"

"You make me so sad," said little Gerda. "Your scent is so strong, I can't help thinking of the dead girls! Ah — is little Kay really dead? The roses have been under the earth, and they say he isn't!"

"*Kling, klang!*" went the hyacinth bells. "We're not ringing for little Kay, we don't even know him! We're only singing our song — the only one we know!"

So Gerda went to the buttercup, bright among its shining green leaves. "You are a little bright sun," said Gerda. "Tell me, do you know where I can find my playfellow?" And the buttercup shone out so lovely and turned up its face to Gerda. What sort of a song could the buttercup sing? It was certainly not about Kay.

"It was the first day of spring and a little courtyard was filled with the warmth of God's good sunshine. The sunbeams slid down the white wall of the next-door house, close by grew the first yellow flowers, shining gold in the warm sunbeams. An old grandmother was outside in her chair and her granddaughter, a poor, pretty servant girl, home on a short visit, kissed the old lady. There was gold, heart's gold, in the blessing of that kiss.

"There you are," said the buttercup. "That's my little story!"

"My poor old granny!" said Gerda. "She's sure to be longing for me and sad for me, just as she was for little Kay. But I'll soon come home again and bring Kay with me. It's no use me asking these flowers, they only know their own little songs and tell me nothing at all." And she caught up her little skirt so she could run faster, but as she jumped over the jonquil it touched her leg, and she stopped and looked at the tall yellow flower and asked, "Perhaps you know something?" and she bent down to the jonquil. And what did it say?

"I can see myself! I can see myself!" said the jonquil. "My! My! What a secret I've got! – Up in a little attic room, half-dressed, there's a little dancer. Sometimes she stands on one leg, sometimes on two and then does high-kicks at the whole world – but she's just an optical illusion. She's pouring water from a teapot on to a bit of stuff she's holding – her bodice. Cleanliness! What a good thing! Her white dress is hanging on a hook and she's washed that in the teapot too and spread it on the roof to dry. She puts it on, with a saffron-yellow scarf round her neck, which makes the dress whiter. One leg up in the air! See how she struts on just one stalk! I can see myself! I can see myself!"

"I can't bother myself with all that," said Gerda, "it doesn't tell me a thing!" – and she ran to the end of the garden. The gate was locked, but she shook the rusty catch till it came loose and the gate sprang open, and little Gerda ran out barefoot into the wide world. She looked back three times but no one came after her, and when she couldn't run any more she sat down on a big stone and looked about her. The summer was over; it was late autumn – and that was something that you'd never notice in the beautiful garden where the sun was always shining, and all seasons' flowers bloomed together.

"Lordy, what a time I've been!" said little Gerda. "Autumn already! I mustn't rest any longer!"– and she got up to go on.

Oh, how tired and sore her little feet were, and how cold and bleak everything round about. The long leaves of the willow were all yellow and a damp dew dropped

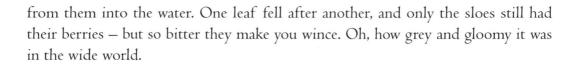
from them into the water. One leaf fell after another, and only the sloes still had their berries — but so bitter they make you wince. Oh, how grey and gloomy it was in the wide world.

FOURTH STORY
WHICH TELLS OF A PRINCE AND A PRINCESS

Gerda had to rest again; then there came hopping across the snow, opposite where she sat, a great big crow, who'd been sitting looking at her for a long time, and nodding his head. Now he said, "*Krah! Krah!* Gohd dah! Gohd dah!" That was the best he could do at speaking but he felt kindly towards the little girl and asked where she was off to, so alone in the wide world. Gerda knew well enough what that word 'alone' meant and felt how big a word it really was, and so she told the crow all about her life and her adventures and asked if he hadn't seen Kay.

And the crow nodded very gravely and said, "Cawed be! Cawed be!"

"Do you think so — really!" cried the little girl, and she nearly throttled the poor crow with kissing him.

"Careful, careful!" said the crow. "I think it might be little Kay, but he's forsaken you now for a princess!"

"Is he living with a princess?" asked Gerda.

"Yes — hark!", said the crow, "but I get so hoarse talking your language. I could tell you so much better in Crow-atian!"

"No, I never learned it," said Gerda. "My granny knew it, and she knew double-Dutch too! But I never learned them!"

"Never mind!" said the crow. "I'll tell you as good as I can, but it'll sound a bit of a mess." And he told her what he knew — which should have sounded like this:

"In the kingdom where we are now there lives a princess who is so amazingly clever that she's read all the newspapers in the world — and, being so clever, she's forgotten them again. Just lately she was sitting on her throne (and that's not all that it's cracked up to be) when she started singing a song that went like this: 'Why oh why shouldn't I be a bride!' 'Well — there's something in that,' she said, so she decided that she would be a bride, but she'd only have a husband who knew how to answer when you talked to him — not one who just stood there looking handsome, because that gets very boring. So she drummed up all her ladies-in-waiting, and when they heard what she had in mind they were delighted. 'What a good idea,' they said, or, 'I was only thinking the same thing the other day.'

"Every word I'm saying is true, you know," said the crow. "I've got a tame sweetheart, who's allowed to go wherever she likes in the palace, and she's told me everything!" (Naturally this sweetheart was also a crow – as they say: 'Birds of a feather flock together.')

"Straight away the newspapers came out with hearts and with the princess's initials all round the edge of the pages. There you could read that any good-looking young man was free to come up to the palace to have a talk with the princess; and the one who talked back so that you could tell he was at home there, and talking at his very best, he was the one the princess would have for a husband! Oh, yes," said the crow, "believe me, it's as true as I'm sitting here – people came streaming up, shoving and pushing and running about, but nobody had any luck on either the first day or the second. They could all talk splendidly when they were outside in the yard, but once they got inside the palace gates and saw the sentries in their silver, and the lackeys on the stairs in their gold, and the big, glittering rooms, they were dumbfounded! And when they stood in front of the throne where the princess was sitting, they couldn't bring themselves to say anything except the last word that she had said, and she didn't need to hear that again. It was just as if the people in there had taken some snuff that had gone to their stomachs and they'd fallen into a doze until they came out in the yard again, and then they could jabber away right enough. There was a queue of people from the town gate to the palace; I was there myself and saw it all," said the crow. "They were hungry and they were thirsty, but they didn't get so much as a glass of lukewarm water from the palace. Some of the brightest ones had brought sandwiches with them, but they wouldn't share them with the chap next door because they thought, 'If he looks hungry then the princess certainly won't have him!'"

"But Kay – little Kay!" asked Gerda. "When did he come? Was he there in the crowd?"

"Give us a chance! Give us a chance! We're getting to him now, because on the third day up to the palace comes a little fellow marching along quite happily without a horse and without a carriage. His eyes shone like yours, he had beautiful long hair, but his clothes were in a terrible state!"

"That was Kay!" shouted Gerda. "Oh – now I've found him!"– and she clapped her hands.

"He had a little knapsack on his back," said the crow.

"No, that must have been his sledge," said Gerda, "because he went off with his sledge."

"That could be so," said the crow, "I didn't look too closely – but this I got from my tame sweetheart, that when he came through the palace gates and saw the sentries in their silver and the lackeys on the stairs in their gold he wasn't the least bit upset, he nodded at them and said, "It must be very boring standing on the stairs like that, I'd sooner go inside!" The rooms glittered with lights; ministers and privy councillors walked about in bare feet carrying golden bowls; anyone would have been overawed. His boots squeaked terribly loudly, but it didn't worry him in the least."

"That's Kay all right," said Gerda. "I know he'd got new boots, I heard them squeaking in Granny's room."

"Yes, they certainly squeaked," said the crow, "and he went cheerfully in to where the princess was sitting on a pearl as big as a spinning wheel, and all the ladies-in-waiting with their maids and their maids' maids, and all the courtiers with their footmen and their footmen's footmen, who all had a page apiece, stood ranged in order, and the nearer they were to the door the prouder they looked. The footman's footman's page-boy who always went about in slippers was hardly to be looked at, standing there so proud in the door!"

"That must have been awful!" said little Gerda. "And did Kay get the princess?"

"If I wasn't a crow I'd have taken her myself, even though I am engaged. He's said to have talked as well as I do when I speak Crow-atian – or so my tame sweetheart says. He was gay and charming; he hadn't come there as a wooer, he'd just come to hear the princess's wise words – and he thought those were fine, and she thought he was fine too!"

"Oh yes! That was Kay," said Gerda. "He was so clever he could do mental arithmetic with fractions. Oh, won't you take me to the palace?"

"Well, that's easily said," said the crow, "but how are we going to do it? I'll talk to my tame sweetheart, she should be able to tell us what to do, because I must tell you this: a little girl like you wouldn't usually be allowed to come in."

"Ooh, I will be, though," said Gerda. "When Kay hears that I'm there he'll come straight out and fetch me!"

"Wait for me over by that stile," said the crow, and he waggled his head and flew off.

It wasn't till late in the afternoon that the crow came back again, "*Rrar! Rrar!*" it said. "She tells me to give you all her good wishes – and here's a little piece of bread for you that she took from the kitchen. They've got bread enough there, and you must be hungry! It just won't be possible for you to come into the palace with those bare feet, the sentries in their silver and the lackeys in their gold wouldn't stand for it, but don't cry – you'll still get in. My sweetheart knows a little back staircase that goes up to the bedroom, and she knows where she can get the key."

So they went into the garden and along the great avenue where the leaves were falling, one after another, and as the lights in the palace went out, one after another, the crow brought little Gerda to a side door which was open just a crack.

Oh, how Gerda's heart was beating with fear and longing! It was as if she was doing something very wrong, and yet she only wanted to see if little Kay was there. Surely, it must be him, his bright eyes and his long hair were so clear in her mind that she could just see him smiling the way he used to do at home, sitting under the roses. He would surely be glad to see her and hear what a long way she'd come for his sake and know how sad they'd all been at home when he didn't come back. Oh, how frightened and glad she was – both at once!

Now they were on the stairs. A little lamp was burning on a cupboard and in the middle of the floor was the tame crow, turning her head from side to side and looking at Gerda, who curtsied just like her granny had taught her.

"My fiancé has said a lot of nice things about you, little lady," said the tame crow. "Your 'life story', as they call it, is very touching! Now you take the lamp and I will lead the way. We are going straight there because we won't meet anyone."

"But somebody's coming after us already!" said Gerda, as something rushed past her; it was like shadows on the wall: horses with flying manes and slender legs – huntsmen – ladies and gentlemen on horseback.

"Those are only dreams," said the crow. "They come and take the gentry's thoughts out hunting – and a good thing too! They can watch it much better in bed. But if you come to honour and dignity I hope that you'll show me a grateful heart."

"That's not something to babble about!" said the crow from the woods.

Now they came into the first chamber which was hung with rose-red satin and had artificial flowers on the walls. Here the dreams were already rushing past them, but they went so quickly that Gerda couldn't get a sight of all the gentry. Each new room was more magnificent than the one before – it was enough to make you dizzy – and then they got to the bed chamber. Here the ceiling was like a huge palm tree with leaves of glass, precious glass, and in the middle of the floor, hanging from a thick golden stalk, there were two beds which looked like lilies. One was white, and there lay the princess; the other was red, and there Gerda would have to look for little Kay. She bent the red leaves out of the way and there she saw the back of a brown neck – oh, yes, that was Kay! – She called out his name, quite loud, holding the lamp over him – the dreams galloped back into the room again – he woke up, turned his head, and – no, it wasn't little Kay.

It was only the prince's neck that was like him, but he was certainly young and handsome. And then from the white-lily bed the princess looked up, blinking, and asked what was happening. Then little Gerda burst out crying and told them her whole story, with everything that the crows had done for her.

"You poor little thing!" said the prince and the princess, and they praised the crows and told them that they weren't cross with them (but not to do such things too often). Meanwhile, they would have a reward.

"Would you like to go free," asked the princess, "or would you like to have an official appointment as Court Crows with the right to everything that falls on the kitchen floor?"

And both the crows bowed and requested the official appointments, because they were thinking of their old age and they said it was such a good thing to have something "for the old man" (as they put it).

Then the prince got out of his bed and let Gerda go to sleep in it – and he couldn't do more than that, could he? She put her little hands together and thought, "How kind everyone is – men and animals both," and she closed her eyes and fell into a peaceful sleep. The dreams all came flying back in again and they looked like God's angels, and they pulled a little sledge with Kay sitting on it, nodding – but it was all just a dream, and disappeared again as soon as she woke up.

The next day they dressed her from top to toe in silk and velvet. They invited her to stay at the palace and join in the fun, but she just begged for a little horse and carriage and a little pair of boots so that she could drive out into the wide world again to find Kay.

So they gave her both boots and a muff. She was beautifully dressed like this, and when she was ready to leave, a new carriage of pure gold came round to the door, with the coats of arms of the prince and princess glittering on it like stars. The coachman, the footmen and the outriders (for she had outriders as well) sat there with gold crowns on their heads. The prince and the princess themselves helped her into the carriage and wished her good luck, and the crow from the woods, who was now married, came with her for the first three miles. (He sat beside her because he couldn't stand driving backwards.) The other crow stood in the gateway flapping her wings. She didn't go with them because she had a headache from getting that official appointment and then eating too much. Inside, the carriage was lined with sugarcakes, and had fruit and gingerbread nuts on the seat.

"Goodbye! Goodbye!" shouted the prince and the princess, and little Gerda wept, and the crow wept. That's how they went along for the first few miles, then the crow said goodbye too, and that was the saddest parting of all. He flew up into a tree and flapped his black wings as long as he could see the carriage, which shone in the distance like the brightest sunshine.

FIFTH STORY
WHICH TELLS OF A LITTLE ROBBER GIRL

They drove onwards through the dark forest, but the carriage shone out like a flame and it dazzled the robbers' eyes so that they couldn't stand it. "That's gold! That's gold!" they shouted, rushing out, seizing the horses, killing the postillions, the coachman and all the servants, and pulling little Gerda out of the coach.

"She's fat, she's a real delicacy, she's been fattened on nuts!" said the old robber-woman, who had a long, bristly beard and eyebrows that hung down over her eyes. "She'll taste as good as a little fatted lamb! My word, I'll enjoy her for supper!" And she drew out her gleaming knife that glittered enough to give you the heebie-jeebies.

"Yowl!" said the old woman, at the very same moment – bitten in the ear by her own daughter, who was hitched up on her back and who looked so wild and untamed that she was a sight to behold. "You horrible little brat!" said her mother – and she

didn't have time to kill Gerda.

"She's to play with me!" said the little robber-girl. "She's to give me her muff and her pretty little dress and come and sleep in my bed!" And she bit her again so that the robberwoman leapt in the air and turned right round, and all the other robbers laughed and said, "Look at her, dancing with her baby!"

"I want to go in the carriage!" said the little robber-girl — and she must and would have her own way because she was so spoiled and obstinate. So she and Gerda sat inside and they rattled over stumps and brambles deep into the forest. The little robber-girl was the same size as Gerda, but stronger, more broad-shouldered, darker-skinned; her eyes were quite black and looked almost sad. She put her arm round little Gerda's waist and said, "They'll not kill you so long as I'm not cross with you! Are you really a princess?"

"No," said little Gerda, and told her everything that had happened and how fond she was of little Kay.

The robber-girl looked at her with big, serious eyes, nodded her head a little and said, "They'll not kill you — if I really get cross with you I'll do it myself!" And she dried Gerda's tears and put both her hands into the pretty muff that was so soft and warm.

Now the carriage stopped; they were in the middle of the courtyard of the robbers' castle; its walls were split from top to bottom, crows and ravens flew out of various gaping holes, and some big bulldogs, each of which looked as though it could swallow a man, leapt up in the air, but they didn't bark because that was forbidden.

A huge fire was burning in the middle of the stone floor of the great old sooty hall; the smoke drifted about up in the roof looking for somewhere to get out; there was soup boiling in a big cauldron, and hares and rabbits turning on a spit.

"You're to sleep here tonight with me and all my pets!" said the robber-girl, and they got something to eat and drink and took themselves off to a corner where some straw and some rugs were lying. Up above there were about a hundred pigeons roosting on laths and perches — all apparently asleep, but they moved about a bit when the little girls arrived.

"They're all mine," said the little robber-girl, and she quickly grabbed one of the nearest, held it by its legs and shook it so that it flapped its wings. "Kiss her!" she cried and shoved it in Gerda's face. "And look at those forest riff-raff!" she went on, pointing behind a lot of slats that were fixed high up across a hole in the wall.

"They're wood-pigeons, those two. They'd fly off straight away if you didn't keep them properly locked up; and here's my old darling Bae!" – and she dragged out a reindeer by its antlers. It was tethered and had a bright copper ring round its neck. "We've got to keep him locked up too or else he'd be up and away. Every single evening I tickle his neck with my dagger – he's frightened enough of that!" And the little girl pulled a long knife from a crack in the wall and let it slide over the reindeer's neck. The poor beast kicked out with its legs and the robber-girl laughed and pulled Gerda down into her bed.

"Do you even have the knife with you when you're asleep?" asked Gerda, and looked at it, frightened.

"Oh, I always sleep with my knife," said the little robber-girl, "you never know what may happen. But now – tell me again what you told me about little Kay, and why you've gone out into the wide world." And Gerda told it from the beginning, and the wood pigeons cooed up there in their cage and the other pigeons slept. The little robber-girl put her arm round Gerda's neck, held her knife in the other hand and fell asleep (you could hear that); but Gerda couldn't close her eyes for a moment – not knowing if she was to live or die. The robbers sat round the fire, singing and drinking, while the robber-woman turned somersaults. Oh, the little girl found it dreadful to look at.

Then the wood pigeon said, "*Kurre, kurre!* We've seen little Kay. A white chicken was carrying his sledge, he was sitting in the Snow Queen's carriage which flew down across the forest where we lay in our nest. Her cold breath blew on the little ones and they all died except us two; *kurre, kurre!*"

"What are you talking about up there?" cried Gerda. "Where was the Snow Queen going to? Don't you know any more about it?"

"She was probably going to Lapland where there's always snow and ice! But why not ask that reindeer there with the rope around his neck?"

"There's ice and snow there," said the reindeer, "and it's all very fine and splendid! You can run free there across the huge, shining valleys! That's where the Snow Queen has her summer tents, but her stronghold is up towards the North Pole on the island called Spitzbergen!"

"Oh, Kay, little Kay!" sighed Gerda.

"Now you just lie still," said the robber-girl, "else you'll get my knife in your belly!"

Next morning Gerda told her everything the wood pigeon had said, and the little robber-girl looked at her with big, serious eyes, but nodded her head too, and said, "Never mind! Never mind! Do you know where Lapland is?" she asked the reindeer.

"Who'd know better than me?" said the creature, and his eyes lit up at the thought. "I was born and bred there — that's where I ran free across the snowfields."

"Listen!" said the robber-girl to Gerda. "You can see that all the men have gone off, but my ma's still here and she'll be staying. Still, later in the morning she'll have a drink from that big bottle and then have a bit of a snooze; then I'll do something for you!" Then she jumped out of bed, threw her arms round her mother's neck, pulled her beard and said, "Good morning, my dear old nanny-goat!" And her mother pinched her under the nose so that it turned red and blue — but that was all done from pure, loving kindness.

So when the mother had had her drink from the bottle and dropped off into a snooze the robber-girl went to the reindeer and said, "I'm still after tickling your gullet a lot more times with my sharp little knife, because it makes you look funny, but never mind — I'll let you off your rope and help you outside so that you can run off to Lapland. You must really use your legs and take this little girl to the Snow Queen's castle for me — that's where her playfellow is. But then you heard what she said because she spoke loud enough and you were listening!"

The reindeer jumped about for joy. The robber-girl lifted little Gerda up on to it and had the good sense to tie her on, and indeed to give her a little cushion to sit on. "Never mind," she said, "you can have your fur boots because it's getting cold, but I'm keeping the muff while it's so pretty! Still, you won't freeze. Here are my ma's big mittens and they'll almost reach to your elbows; put 'em on! Now your hands look like my ugly old ma's!"

And Gerda wept for joy.

"I can't stand your grizzling," said the little robber-girl. "You ought to be delighted! And here's two rolls and a ham for you so that you won't starve." Both of these were tied behind her on the reindeer. The little robber-girl opened the door, shut up all the big dogs and then cut the rope with her knife and said to the reindeer: "Off you go! But look after the little girl!"

And Gerda stretched out her hands in the big mittens towards the robber-girl and said goodbye, and then the reindeer leapt off over bushes and fallen trees, through

Wolves howled and ravens screeched

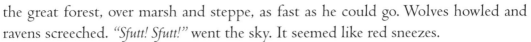
the great forest, over marsh and steppe, as fast as he could go. Wolves howled and ravens screeched. *"Sfutt! Sfutt!"* went the sky. It seemed like red sneezes.

"Those are my dear old Northern Lights!" said the reindeer. "How they flash!" And he ran on faster than ever — night and day. By the time she'd eaten all the rolls and the ham they were in Lapland.

SIXTH STORY
Which tells of the Lapp woman and the Finn woman

They came to a stop at a little house — very ramshackle. The roof sloped down almost to the ground and the doorway was so low that the family had to creep on their stomachs when they wanted to go in or out. No one was at home except for an old Lapp woman who was standing there cooking fish over an oil lamp. The reindeer told her Gerda's story (but his own first of all, because that seemed to him to be more important). Gerda was so perished with cold that she was beyond telling anything.

"Oh — you poor things!" said the Lapp woman. "You've still got a long way to run! You must go over a hundred miles into Finmark — the Snow Queen's staying in the country there, letting off Bengal lights every evening. I'll scribble a few words on a dried codfish (I've not got any paper) and you can take that up there to the Finn woman — she can give you better directions than me."

And now that Gerda was warm again and had had something to eat and drink, the Lapp woman scribbled her few words on the dried codfish, bade Gerda look after it, tied her fast again on the reindeer's back, and off he went. *"Sfutt! Sfutt!"* it said, up in the air, and the whole night the Northern Lights burned with the most beautiful blue; and so they came to Finmark and knocked on the Finn woman's chimney, for there wasn't a door to go in at.

It was so hot inside that the Finn woman herself went about almost naked. She was small and very dirty, and straight away she loosened little Gerda's clothes and took off her mittens and boots, otherwise it would have been too hot for her. She put a chunk of ice on the reindeer's head and read what was written on the codfish. She read it three times and when she had it by heart she dropped the fish into the soup-tureen for it was a tasty morsel and she wasn't one to waste things.

Now the reindeer first of all told his own story, then little Gerda's, and the Finn woman blinked her wise eyes but said nothing.

"You are so wise," said the reindeer. "I know you can bind all the winds of the world with a thread of cotton; if a sailor unties the first knot he gets a good wind, the second and it blows more strongly, the third and fourth and there's a storm fit to blow down the forests. Won't you give the little girl a drink so that she'll have the strength of twelve to overcome the Snow Queen?"

"The strength of twelve," said the Finn woman, "oh yes, that will do a lot of good!" And she went over to a shelf, took down a great, rolled-up skin, and unrolled it. Strange characters were written on it and the Finn woman read till the sweat dripped from her forehead. But the reindeer begged again so hard for little Gerda, and Gerda looked at the Finn woman so beseechingly, with her eyes full of tears, that the Finn woman began to blink her own eyes and took the reindeer off into a corner where she whispered to him, while she put a fresh lump of ice on his head.

"Little Kay is at the Snow Queen's right enough, and everything there suits him very well so that he thinks it's the best place in the world; but that's because he's got a splinter of glass in his heart and a little speck of glass in his eye. Without you getting that out first, he'll never be human again and the Snow Queen will keep her power over him."

"But can't you give little Gerda something that will give her power over the lot of them?"

"I can't give her any greater power than she already has! Don't you see how strong it is? Don't you see how men and beasts have had to serve her, how far she's travelled in the world on her two bare feet? She mustn't learn what this power is from us, it comes from her heart, it comes from her being a sweet, innocent child. If she can't get into the Snow Queen's herself and take the glass from little Kay, then there's nothing we can do to help. Two miles from here is the start of the Snow Queen's garden. You can carry the little girl there and put her down by the big bush standing in the snow with red berries on it. Don't stand around chatting, but come back here as quick as possible!" And so the Finn woman lifted little Gerda on to the reindeer and he ran off as fast as he could.

"Oh, I haven't got my boots! I haven't got my mittens!" shouted little Gerda as she found the cold cutting into her, but the reindeer didn't dare stop. He ran till he came to the big bush with the red berries and there he set Gerda down, kissed her on the mouth while big, glistening tears ran down the creature's cheeks — and then he ran off back again as fast as he could. There stood poor Gerda, without shoes, without gloves, in the middle of icy, freezing Finmark.

She ran forward as well as she could, and then along came a whole regiment of snowflakes. But they weren't falling from the sky, for that was clear and lit up with the Northern Lights; they were running along the ground, and the nearer they came the bigger they grew. Gerda still remembered how large and artistically manufactured they looked when she saw the snowflakes through the magnifying glass, but now they were altogether different — big and frightening. They were alive. They were the Snow Queen's outlying guards, and they took on the strangest shapes: some looked like great ugly hedgehogs, others like a huge tangle of snakes, darting their heads out, and others were like small, stumpy bears with their hair sticking out. They were all glittering white, all living snowflakes.

Then little Gerda said her Lord's Prayer, and the cold was so bitter that she could see her own breath coming out of her mouth like smoke. These puffs of breath grew thicker and thicker and turned into small, bright angels who got bigger and bigger as they touched the ground. They all had helmets on their heads, and shields and spears in their hands. More and more of them came, and when Gerda had finished her prayer she was surrounded by a whole legion of them. They thrust their spears into the terrible snowflakes so that they split into a hundred pieces, and little Gerda went forward safely and in peace. The angels stroked her on her hands and on her feet so that she felt less and less how cold it was, and so she came up quickly to the Snow Queen's palace.

But now let's first see what Kay is up to. He's certainly not thinking about little Gerda, and least of all that she's standing there outside the palace.

SEVENTH STORY
WHAT HAPPENED IN THE SNOW QUEEN'S PALACE AND WHAT HAPPENED AFTERWARDS

The walls of the palace were made of driven snow, and the doors and windows of piercing wind. It had over a hundred rooms, all piled up with snow; the biggest was many miles long, and everything was lit up by the great Northern Lights — so vast, so empty, so icy cold and glittering. You'd never find any merry-making here, not even so much as a modest dance for the bears with the storm blowing tunes for them and the polar bears walking on their back legs and showing off their airs and graces; never a little game of cards with licking of chops and slapping of paws; never a little gossipy coffee morning for the white lady foxes. The halls of the Snow Queen were vast, cold and empty. The Northern Lights burned so exactly to time that you could tell exactly when they were at their highest and when at their lowest. In the middle of this endless, empty hall of snow there was a frozen lake: it had split into thousands of pieces, but each piece was so exactly like the next that it looked as though they'd been made by machine; and in the middle of this there sat the Snow Queen — when she was at home — and she said that she was sitting in the Mirror of Reason and that it was the best one, indeed the only one, in the world.

Little Kay was blue — really, almost black — with cold, but he didn't notice it for she had kissed the cold shivers away from him and his heart was no better than a lump of ice. He was going about dragging some flat, sharp-edged blocks of ice which he set down in various ways as though he was trying to make something out of them. (It was like the rest of us do with what they call a Chinese Puzzle — making patterns by pushing about small flat pieces of wood.) Kay was going about making patterns too — altogether very intricate ones, which were part of 'A Game of Reason on Ice'. In his eyes these patterns were most remarkable and of absolutely the highest importance — that was because of the speck of glass that was stuck in his eye! He laid out complete patterns to form words, but he could never manage to set down the word that he wanted, the word ETERNITY, for the Snow Queen had said, "If you can work out that pattern for me then you shall be your own master and I shall give you the whole world for a present, and a new pair of skates." But he couldn't do it.

"Now I'm away to the warm countries," said the Snow Queen. "I'm going to take a quick look at the black saucepans!" (These were the volcanoes that we call Etna and Vesuvius.) "I shall whiten them over a bit, that's what they need — good for the lemons and the grapes!" And away flew the Snow Queen, leaving Kay sitting there all alone in the vast, empty miles of the hall of ice, looking at his blocks of ice and

He laid out complete patterns to form words

thinking so that he crackled inside. He sat there so stiff and still that you'd think he was frozen himself.

It was then that little Gerda stepped into the palace through the great gate of piercing wind; but she recited the Evening Prayer and the winds lay down as if they would go to sleep, and she stepped into the vast, cold, empty hall. Then she saw Kay, recognised him, flung her arms round his neck, held him so tight and shouted, "Kay! Dear little Kay! I've found you!"

But he sat perfectly still, stiff and cold; then little Gerda wept hot tears, and they fell down on to his breast, seeped into his heart, melted the lump of ice and consumed the little splinter of mirror that was there. He looked at her and she sang the hymn:

Little Jesus walked with us,
Little Jesus talked with us,
Down in the valley where the roses grow.

Then Kay burst into tears; he cried so hard that the speck of mirror was washed out of his eye; he recognised her and shouted joyfully, "Gerda! Dear little Gerda! Why have you taken so long? And where have I been?" And he looked about. "Ooh, but it's cold here! Ooh, but it's all big and empty!" And he clung on to Gerda and she laughed and cried for joy. It was all so glorious that the blocks of ice themselves danced about for joy, and when they were tired and laid themselves down they exactly made up those letters which the Snow Queen had told him to work out — when he should be his own master and when she would give him the world as a present and a new pair of skates.

And Gerda kissed his cheeks and they recovered their bloom; she kissed his eyes and they shone like her own; she kissed his hands and his feet and he was whole and alive. The Snow Queen could come home when she would: his order of release was written there in shining blocks of ice.

And they took each other by the hand and made their way out of the great palace, talking about Old Granny and the roses up on the roof; and wherever they walked the winds dropped away to nothing and the sun shone out. And as they got nearer the bush with the red berries, there stood the reindeer waiting for them. He'd brought another young reindeer with him, a doe with full udders, and she let the children drink her warm milk and kissed them on the mouth. Then they carried Kay and

Gerda first to the Finn woman, where they got themselves warm in the hot little room and were given instructions about their journey home, then to the Lapp woman, who had sewed them some new clothes and put her sledge in order.

And the reindeer and the young doe ran beside them, keeping them company, to the borders of that land, where the first green shoots were beginning to show, and here they said goodbye to the reindeer and the Lapp woman. "Farewell! Farewell!" they all cried to each other.

And the first small birds began to twitter, the forest bore green buds — and out of it there came riding a splendid horse that Gerda knew (it had been harnessed to the gold carriage) and a young girl with a bright-red cap on her head and pistols in front of her. That, of course, was the little robber-girl, who was bored with staying at home and who was making first for the North, and later for any other part if that didn't suit her. She recognised Gerda straight away and Gerda recognised her and there was much rejoicing.

"You're a fine fellow to go on a jaunt!" she said to little Kay. "I'd like to know if you deserve to have people running off to the end of the world just for you!"

But Gerda stroked her cheek and asked after the prince and the princess.

"They've gone off to foreign parts," said the robber-girl.

"But what about the crow?" asked little Gerda.

"Oh, the crow's dead," was the answer. "His tame sweetheart is a widow and goes about with a bit of wool round her leg. She's dreadfully sorry for herself, but it's all pretence. But now, tell me how things went with you and how you got hold of him."

And Gerda and Kay both told her.

"So snip-snap-snout, the tale's told out," said the robber-girl, and took them both by the hand and promised that if she ever came to their town she'd come up and pay them a visit — and off she rode into the wide world. But Kay and Gerda walked hand in hand and as they went along the Spring blossomed about them with flowers and green leaves. Church bells were ringing and they recognised the high towers, the great city where they lived. And they went in and along to the grandmother's door, up the staircase, into the room, where everything was just the same as before, and the clock said, "Tick! Tick!" as its hands went round. But as they came through the door they realised that they had grown up.

The roses across the roof gutter were flowering in at the open window, and there stood the children's little stools, and Kay and Gerda each sat down on their own one and held each other's hands. The Snow Queen's cold, empty majesty was forgotten, like a dark dream. Old Granny sat in God's good sunshine, reading aloud from her Bible, '*Except ye become as little children, ye shall not enter the Kingdom of Heaven.*'

And Kay and Gerda looked into each other's eyes and all at once they understood the old hymn:

Little Jesus walked with us,
Little Jesus talked with us,
Down in the valley where the roses grow.

There the two of them sat: grown-up and yet children – children at heart – and it was summer, warm, beautiful summer.

AFTERWORD BY THE TRANSLATOR

Many of Andersen's stories were published as *eventyr*, a word that has usually been translated as 'fairy tale' and has regularly led to them being anthologised as such, especially in compendia such as *The Fairy Tales of Grimm and Andersen*. For the most part though, they were nothing of the sort. Traditional tales have no 'author', and versions of them can be found higgledy-piggledy all over the place. In contrast, Andersen's tales were the invention of Andersen himself, set down in a way that reflected the manner of a speaking voice – his voice. That was specific in a way that the language of traditional tales was not. However, in some cases, especially early on in their publication, Andersen did draw on a memory or even a knowledge of tales in the folk tradition, elements of which he incorporated in the story he was inventing.

In this revised version of *Michael Foreman Illustrates: Hans Andersen's Fairy Tales*, the stories selected for the first edition of 1976 have been retained. However, by placing them in the chronological order of their original Danish publication we can show something of the growing originality of his writing. The following notes provide both the title and date of their first Danish appearance and a note where a traditional source may play some part in the composition. Acknowledgement must be made to Elias Bredsdorff for identifying some of these sources in his biography of Andersen, published in 1975. In one instance only have we departed from the chronological ordering. The story of 'The Snow Queen' is deemed by both translator and publisher to be of such beauty and distinction that it has been placed at the end of the collection.

Brian Alderson
Richmond in the North Riding of Yorkshire
February 2013

THE STORY OF THE TRANSLATOR

Brian Alderson

Many years ago, Brian Alderson got the sack from a job in the book trade. Recently married and with a small son yowling in his cradle, he seized the first job on offer and went to work for a bookseller who specialised in children's books. It didn't seem a very big decision at the time, but it more or less determined the rest of his working life.

At root, he supposes, Brian found himself drawn to the way in which children's books offered their small customers such a feast of experiences, whether showing you what can be done to an apple pie or what might happen to you if you fell down a rabbit hole. There were riches here for everyone, opening a way to a lifetime of reading. So Brian left the bookshop and followed the example of the man who 'jumped on a horse and rode off in all directions'. He edited books; lectured on 'Children's Literature' in both England and the United States; organised several national exhibitions on the subject; and worked as Children's Books Editor at *The Times* for over 30 years.

In all this though it was never far from his mind that storytellers represented the very source of a free and unhampered children's literature – after all, were not Sheherazade and Mother Goose and Mother Bunch present when children's books were born? Brian took great pleasure in telling traditional tales to his own and to other children and, having a passable knowledge of German and Danish, he set about bringing the tales made famous by the Brothers Grimm and by Hans Christian Andersen into storyteller's English. As he says in his Afterword here, he owes it to those old folk, sat round their firesides, to do justice to their speaking voices. Whether he has done so or not, the readers or listeners must decide.

ABOUT THE ILLUSTRATOR

Michael Foreman

Michael Foreman grew up in the fishing village of Pakefield in Suffolk. His mother ran the Pakefield newsagent, and it was during his daily paper round that Michael met a teacher from Lowestoft Art School who encouraged him to attend his Saturday art class for children. Michael's talent was obvious, so his teacher suggested that he come to the art school two afternoons a week, eventually attending the art school full time.

Michael's first book, *The General*, was published while he was still a student at the Royal College of Art in London. Since then, Michael has become one of the greatest creators of children's books of recent times. An intrepid traveller, he makes hundreds of sketches whilst abroad which then inspire his books. He has illustrated collections of fairy tales and legends from all over the world, as well as the works of Dickens, Shakespeare, Roald Dahl, Rudyard Kipling, Robert Louis Stevenson and many others. He has also designed Christmas stamps for the Post Office.

Michael has written and illustrated an amazing collection of books himself, many based on his personal experiences of growing up during the Second World War. As his local beach was sprinkled with mines and covered with barbed wire, bombsites became his playground. His work often returns to issues of war, the environment and, above all, a child's need for freedom and adventure. The autobiographical *War Boy* won the Kate Greenaway Medal, and *War Game* won the Nestlé Smarties Book Prize.

Michael is married and has three sons. He spends most of his time in London, but regularly visits St Ives in Cornwall where he has a studio. As a result, many of his books feature the land and seascapes of Cornwall.

Notes on the Text

The Tinderbox *Fyrtøiet* (1835), owing elements (but not the dogs) to both *Aladdin* and the Grimms' *The Blue Light*. This translation first published in a new edition of Andrew Lang's *Yellow Fairy Book* (1980). Other translations here by Brian Alderson in either that book or the *Pink Fairy Book* (1982) are simply designated below as either 'Lang *Yellow*' or 'Lang *Pink*'

Little Claus and Big Claus *Lille Claus og store Claus* (1835). Elias Bredsdorff points out a close similarity of this tale to both a Danish and a Norwegian story. (Lang *Yellow*)

The Princess on the Pea *Prindsessen paa Ærten* (1835). Bredsdorff notes a Swedish tale where the test is used to prove a visiting princess to be an impostor. (Lang *Yellow*)

Thumbelina *Tommelise* (1835). Andersen's first venture into creating a wholly original fantasy tale.

The Little Mermaid *Den lille Havfrue* (1837). The imaginative thrust of the narrative probably owes something to a reading of De La Motte Fouqué's novel *Undine*. The present translator's dislike of the sentimental ending of Andersen's tale has led him to interpolate a minor modification at that point, not affecting the original text.

The Emperor's New Clothes *Keiserens nye Klæder* (1837). Andersen claims a source for this story in his reading (in German) of a Spanish story, identified by Bredsdorff as a tale in the *Libro de Patronio* by the Infante Don Juan Manuel. (Lang *Yellow*)

The Steadfast Tin Soldier *Den standhaftige Tinsoldat* (1838) The earliest example of Andersen's genius at imbuing toys and household objects with a vibrant life of their own. (Lang *Yellow*)

The Wild Swans *De vilder Svane* (1838). See also two cognate folktales in the Grimms' collection: 'The Six Swans' and 'The Seven Ravens'.

The Swineherd *Svinedrengen* (1842). (Lang *Yellow*.) See also the cognate Grimm story 'King Throstlebeard', as translated in *Michael Foreman illustrates the Brothers Grimm* pp.113–8.

The Nightingale *Nattergalen* (1844). (Lang *Yellow*)

The Ugly Duckling *Den grimme Ælling* (1844). Universally recognised as Andersen's proud claim that he, "though born in a duck-yard", had "come out of a swan's egg".

The Red Shoes *De røde Skoe* (1845). A tiny addition to the description of the old soldier has been added, implying that the man who magically initiates the little girl's dreadful fate might be the storyteller himself. Young ladies don't always escape without suffering in Andersen's stories.

The Old House *Det gamle Huus* (1848).

The Little Match-Girl *Den lille Pige med Svovlstickkerne* (1848).

The Dung Beetle *Skarnbassen* (1861).

The Snowman *Sneemanden* (1861). (Lang *Pink*)

The Snow Queen; an adventure in seven stories *Sneedronningen; et Eventyr I syv Historier* (1845). (Lang *Pink*)